The
War Artist

Steven Kelly

Scribner

First published in Great Britain by Scribner, 1999
This edition first published by Scribner, 2000
An imprint of Simon & Schuster UK Ltd
A Viacom Company

1 3 5 7 9 10 8 6 4 2

Simon & Schuster UK Ltd
Africa House
64-78 Kingsway
London WC2B 6AH

Simon & Schuster Australia
Sydney

A CIP catalogue record for this book is available from the British Library

ISBN 0-684-85132-6

Typeset by SX Composing DTP, Rayleigh, Essex
Printed and bound in Finland by WSOY

Praise for *The War Artist*

Amazon.co.uk Customer comments
A reader from Liverpool

'This is a book which gives you hope for the future of literature in England – an original, brilliantly written and very passionate piece of writing from an author we'll surely hear a lot about in the future. Charles Monk is the war artist of the title, a larger than life figure whose loves are as unconstrained and uninhibited as his life, but whose life is empty since the death of the woman he loved. Retired to London he has the demons of his past still to face and, true to life, redemption comes in the most obscure way. This isn't a book for everyone. At times it's elitist in tone and you need to have lived a bit to appreciate its emotional power. But for anyone interested in serious, ideas-led literary fiction The War Artist is a must-read. Highly recommended'

Bol.com Customer comments
A reader

'A tour de force of Hemingwayesque proportions. Kelly's characters are by turns savage and beautiful. A must read with the intensity of a slaughter house filmed as a European art movie. Unmissible'

'Ranging from the Sorbonne to Khe Sah and modern-day London, The War Artist is written in a sparse, economical style which deftly sidesteps the danger of pretension whilst encompassing classical mythology, obsessive love, the relationship between art and life, underage sex and spaghetti westerns. And you can't say that about very many novels'
SPIKE MAGAZINE, ONLINE

Praise for *The Moon Rising*

'This is an accomplished first novel'
TIME OUT

'There is a dramatic intensity about this work, as tempers rise and nerves fray, and Kelly's precise, measured prose perfectly evokes the encroaching avalanches, the shattered glass, the stinging snow, and the emotional vacuity of his young protagonist. The writing, seemingly matter-of-fact, deceives with its calm, adding menace to an already disturbing depiction of fractured lives and unarticulated desires'
SUNDAY TIMES

'This quietly menacing novella is an assured performance'
CHIC MAGAZINE

'Kelly gives the "unfailing sense of being young" – and in love – with all the skill and precision of a true professional'
PENELOPE FITZGERALD, EVENING STANDARD

Praise for *Invisible Architecture*

'Striking ... impressive ... polished'
INDEPENDENT

'Elegant and original ... beautifully crafted, without a word out of place or a sentence too many'
TIME OUT

'Stark, economical and elegant'
SUNDAY TIMES

'Brilliant and disturbing ... These extravagant stories of love and death are told in the quietest, most economical manner'
PENELOPE FITZGERALD, EVENING STANDARD

Athene lifted the thick veil of darkness from their eyes.

– HOMER

PROLOGUE

He woke to find himself lying on his back. His head was held immobile in some kind of vice, his jaw braced with a metal clamp attached to his teeth. His torso and limbs were strapped tightly to the cold, hard surface beneath him.

He could feel nothing, realised quickly that they had injected his face with a local anaesthetic. He was strangely relieved: there would be no more pain.

His tongue was thick and lifeless in his mouth, his cheeks swollen. The back of his head where he had been struck throbbed dully.

The surgeon loomed over him, a green silhouette against the bright surgical lamps. He dripped drops from a pipette into his eyes.

The woman's outline appeared in the surgeon's place. She peered at him. He wanted to ask her why, but could make no sound and besides, he knew why: they had discussed it, and for her part she was simply fulfilling her side of a bargain into which he had entered freely.

He had no regrets.

She went away again.

'Are you sure this is the best way?' she asked.

'I'm sure. It'll destroy the retina, the optic nerve, everything.'

The surgeon held open the eyelids of his left eye with latex-gloved fingers. On the periphery of his vision, he could see a syringe bearing towards him. There was a sudden pressure inside his eyeball, a greying of the sight in his left eye.

The surgeon held open the eyelids of his right eye and again, the syringe, the pressure.

And then his world was black.

ONE

LIFE AS AN INTERFACE BETWEEN DIVERSE NEUROSES (SELF–PORTRAIT WITH FLOWERS)

1967. Oil on canvas. 124 × 87.5 cm. Portrait of the artist grimacing. Tate Gallery, London.

NOTES: Fascinating study in the human experience of pain, the title contains a pun on 'neuroses' (new roses). The portrait was painted whilst, out of picture, the artist clutched tightly by their stems a large bouquet of roses, deliberately impaling himself on the thorns – and suffering near-fatal blood-poisoning as a result. The shadowy figure in the background almost certainly represents Miriam Janssen. Regarded by Monk as a work of war art, it was painted at Olaf Janssen's residence in Tangiers at the end of the artist's first tour of Vietnam and reflects Monk's motif feelings of being unable to engage emotionally in the suffering he so frequently witnessed. Donated to the Tate by Lars Janssen, 1973, in compensation for damage caused by Monk to his own portrait of William Calley (see under: *Whatever it Takes to Numb the Pain*).

Charles Monk: An Artist at War by Claude Tartaro.
London: Privately printed, 199-. Page 23.

The Republic occupies a nineteen-thirties building on Russia Street in the west of London, not far from Notting Hill Gate a little further west or Bayswater Road to the south or Westbourne Grove to the north or Queensway to the east. From the outside the building has the austere functionality of its period, but a certain robust grandeur goes with this, and a quality of permanence and calm. It is a building which has meditated the years, followed the breath of the city itself to find its still point.

The Republic's owners, when they reopened the building after twelve years of closure and neglect, chose to retain the exterior's faded aspect. The brickwork remains encrusted with pigeon droppings and soot. Paint flakes from windowsills and eaves. Only the insides of window-panes are cleaned; their outsides are drizzled with grey rivulets and visibility changes with the seasons. Roof slates were replaced as a concession to common sense, and the guttering and pipework is new. Every morning a cleaner swabs the pavement outside the kitchens, and another scrubs the steps which lead to the club's main doorway.

Most of the building's ground floor is taken up by an entrance hall with marble staircases winding up the walls on either side. The entrance hall itself is spartan, with neither paintings nor furniture or decoration of any type. The white marble floor is bare. The space smells faintly of lemon and iron. As one ascends either staircase there is a sense of removal: an optical effect. One might feel that one is going down and not up. It is an effect which is reinforced when, at the top of each staircase, one finds the three steps which descend from the landing into the Republic's foyer, a tiny, richly carpeted and dimly lit room, its closeness at odds with the airy asceticism of what has gone before.

In the foyer names and coats are taken and from there one ascends a further staircase and enters either left the restaurant, or right the Exchequer Room. The Exchequer Room is a large, warmly cluttered salon whose ceiling-to-floor windows face out over Russia Street, framed by heavy, faded red drapes which are drawn shut only in the depths of the coldest winter. In summer the windows are thrown open to let the noise of Russia Street echo in off the walls of the mansion blocks opposite.

The room is furnished with an eclectic mix of sofas and armchairs arranged around diverse coffee tables, many of them workshop pieces unsuited to this type of commercial use. The bar which extends along fully half of the room's south wall is cool and modern in design, an expanse of steel and black-stained wood. On the walls hang many paintings by well-known twentieth-century artists: Picasso, Bacon, Warhol, Pollock, Freud, Kokoschka, Hockney, even a Hitler, but that bought and displayed as a joke which has long since worn thin.

At five o'clock one Thursday afternoon in August a man wearing dark sunglasses and an expensive suit sat in the north-west corner of the Exchequer Room, a corner coveted for its proximity in summer to a window and in winter to the huge fireplace set in the west wall. Charles Monk, curator of the Republic's art collection and godfather to the wealthiest non-identical twins on the planet, had eaten well in the Republic's restaurant: an English lunch of calf's brains in black butter; a mixed grill of liver and kidneys and steak, skuets; an eel pie, roast potatoes and greens and swede mash and gravy, all washed down with stout ale and champagne; then gooseberry tart and a great deal of cream. And now he had drunk port and coffee and smoked a cigar.

He was a large man, not obese but tall and thickly muscled after a lifetime of adventuring. He occupied his armchair with heavily-laden discomfort, twisting in his seat and shifting his weight from side to side. The armchair was new, custom-made by a shop in Surrey and delivered just a few days earlier; it was well-sized and sturdy, its seat deep. It was upholstered in worn brown leather which had been rescued from a woodworm-ridden sofa from another part of the building. After his old armchair had fallen apart Monk had broken half-a-dozen chairs and stools and for a few days he had been reduced to standing at the bar, his feet and ankles swelling under his weight and in the heat to twice their normal size.

It had not been a hot summer but the weather that week had been hot and it was a hot day on this day, too.

The armchair made him think of someone he once knew, William 'Buck' Rogers, a veteran of wars and mutinies and storms and shipwrecks, captain of the *Ringhorn* and the man who had shown Monk the sea thirty-five years before.

'There are two things a man needs,' Rogers had said to

him once. 'A man needs a belt to hold up his pants, and he needs an armchair he can call his own.'

Every man should have an armchair he can call his own. Monk had not understood that at the time, but then he had not been a man at the time: fourteen, just a boy, piss and vinegar in jars, no brains to speak of, a tall, awkward youth with fine hands, a clear eye, a head full of dreams, a nervous need for fear, no knowledge of real suffering or pain.

Monk understood it now: there was truth here: what is a man if he has no armchair he can call his own? less than a man: little more than a beetle: beetles do not have armchairs; this gave him comfort: a rule by which to measure other men.

He shook these thoughts from his head, a nervous habit which he knew made him look like a drunk, but he did not care and anyway the Exchequer Room was almost deserted, just the Republic's sole poet at his usual table at the other end of the room: jug of coffee, blue haze, half-a-dozen notebooks, a mugful of yellow pencils, yellowing skin and hair; they had not spoken in years, never would again, but they knew each other, exchanged the odd nod; the poet had even written a poem about him once, many years before in Paris, a homoerotic fantasy which a smaller man might have considered libellous at the time, but which Monk treasured still for the loneliness and repression and fear that it betrayed; did the poet have an armchair he could call his own? it seemed difficult to believe that he might, and yet Monk imagined that he must, perhaps a very old armchair with worn, yellowing upholstery and wooden arms dotted with cigarette burns. Not much of an armchair, but an armchair all the same and one the poet would have made his own by force of circumstance or habit; were he to visit the poet's home, the poet would claim his own armchair to sit in: an affirmation of the fact that it was his home, that Monk was the guest, or intruder; perhaps the poet would do as Monk would do: sling a leg over the wooden arm of his armchair, just to reinforce his claim; and down the back of his armchair, between the seat pillow and the backrest, what there? Shreds of tobacco and dust and old coins, of course, what else? Cat hairs – the poet surely had a cat or two – and feathers or crumbles of foam rubber, perhaps a yellow pencil sharpened to a stub, or a book: a slim volume of poems, the poet's own, his sole remaining copy of his first volume, long thought lost, its loss long grieved.

Monk shook these thoughts from his head. He shifted his weight from left to right, rubbed the knuckles of his right hand against the underside of his chin. He was full but still hungry: a familiar dull ache at the back of his throat which made him want to gag. Only food or drink would relieve it, and then only for a few minutes at a time. He shifted his weight from right to left, wondered what he might drink or eat, decided to wait.

The hunger had got worse. There were weekends when he could not sleep, but would go to Soho and make his way from restaurant to bar to pub to restaurant, eating, drinking, drinking, eating. It was affecting his work. Every time he prepared a canvas, mixed some paints, the hunger would attack him, forcing him to eat until he could eat no more. Then he would vomit and eat again.

'Like a fucking Roman at a banquet,' he said to the room.

The poet glanced up, used to these outbursts but resentful of them, Monk was sure. He did not care.

'I have no time for anally retentive poets,' he said.

The poet kept his head down, ears burning. The fumes layered the air.

He was waiting for a blind man.

He had found Pete Dixon the way he had found all the blind men. He had called the RNIB and pretended to be a blind man himself; he had told the woman on the end of the telephone that he had recently lost his sight. Was there a support group in London he could join? He had not felt like explaining who or why or what. The lie was easier.

It had seemed like a good idea at the time. He had turned his back on war. He wanted now to subject his own art and life to a personal, intellectual exploration. It had seemed like a fine idea to search out some blind men. If he could explain to them, if they could explain to him, half the job would be done. They would share with one another their perceptions of art, of colour and light and shade and visual texture, perspective. Monk wished to learn to see as they saw, to understand how a blind man might experience a Dali or a Braque. Or a Monk. By learning to give description in detail, he thought, by condensing pictures into ideas, he would learn new ways to express his own experiences of art and war.

It was a stupid idea, but he had learnt from his mistake: we are all as blind as we want to be. Not much of a lesson, an education in his own lack of vision, no more.

*

There were ten of them. They became his friends, not all of them and not close friends, not friends he would think to ask anything of beyond occasional companionship, the odd opinion. Casual friends whom he could live without but who enriched his life in small, unexpected ways, the way a tree can enrich your life, or a particular summer evening that you remember well: ice-cold beer, a beautiful woman's smile just for you, the song of birds or the snarling chatter of squirrels, water running from a tap.

Each of them was different, but he could not help but think of them as the Blind Men, his Blind Men, an ironic-collective Enlightening of Blind Men. Pete Dixon was one of the best: a good listener when it was needed, a jovial conversationalist always, an unusual mix: Monk's kind of guy: the kind of guy Monk might have liked to have been but he was not good at listening, would lose track of conversations, miss names, places, birthdays, the existence of wives and children: a poor friend to have, though a friend who would cover your back, he could say that much for himself: a friend who would take a bullet for you if that was what it came to, or an arrow.

Reaching inside his shirt, fingering the scar tissue on his shoulder, knobbly and profound: a wound that took eight months to heal: excrement on the arrowhead: the constant seepage of pus, the fevers. They said it might never heal: wound-management: keep it clean but get used to it. In the end an old Masai herdsman, no teeth, bloodstained lips, cut the wound and applied a poultice to it: cow dung and herbs, congealed blood and milk, other things: one week later the wound was closed.

Monk had painted that Masai herdsman, painted him

without his knowing it, stolen his image and sold it. Years later he sent the money he received for the painting to the man's family. It was not enough: he tracked down the painting, a six-month search, bought it for five times its real value, bought it and burnt it, a private ceremony: let the man's soul rest, let his own mind have peace in this matter at least, a token of gratitude and respect for the man who healed this wound, of forgiveness for the man or woman who had caused it. A cleansing.

But there was that need for contempt: small, fleeting contempts, the deeper contempt: having washed your soul, the need to become unclean again so you may wash again: nothing like another man's blood and shit and death in his eyes and his entrails in your hands for that. A young journalist, late twenties, mild-mannered, intellectual, polite, only two years ago now, a young journalist in a whole war full of earnest young journalists, guts pooling around her feet, impaled on the branch of a tree, thrown there by the force of the explosion. Monk had watched her die, could not move her, had no weapon with which to dispatch her. He had held her hand and kissed her on the lips: a chaste kiss but he had felt aroused, he could not deny that: was tempted to reach into the mess of her stomach and feel its warmth even as her life ebbed away: the exact moment when enough became more than enough.

Even then he had stayed for one more year, a war junkie, unable to tear himself from it, transfixed and blinded, rabbit-like, by the cold inferno of suffering around him.

Enough was more than enough: no more war.

Monk closed his eyes and rested back in his armchair. He breathed deeply and tried not to swallow. His saliva was unlit napalm on the back of his tongue. He ground his teeth. Sparks flew from them.

He heard the poet shift in his seat. He poked his tongue into his cheek: he would need to keep a straight face. He said loudly: '*Chaque fois que j'ai lu Shakspeare, il m'a semblé que je déchiquette la cervelle d'un jaguar.*'

Monk opened his eyes to watch as the poet paled, stood and ran from the room, almost fell as he caught his jacket pocket on the doorknob on the way out. There was the sound of old, dry tweed seams tearing. The shredded remains of a jaguar's brains spilled on to the floor and disappeared into the woodworm trails etched in the old oak boards.

Monk laughed. He closed his eyes again and more quietly, almost to himself, he said: '*La poésie doit être faite par tous. Non par un.*'

The night before, he had got drunk with another Blind Man, Simon Morton. Monk had sent a car to pick Simon Morton up from his Islington home and bring him to one of the new bars that had opened in Soho over the summer, a cool bar with loud music and loud kids drinking bottled beer and smoking joints without a care in the world. Monk's kind of place, Simon Morton's too.

'Like the trenches, just less blood,' he had said to Simon Morton. Simon Morton had laughed: another idiot who wished he had been born half a century earlier and fought in The Big One, writing poetry while he was at it, no idea of what it would really have been like to die in Flanders, or worse, perhaps, survive.

Monk had ordered splits of Krug which they drank from the bottle but no one got the joke, or if they did they did not laugh: the young: so fucking serious he could die. They moved on to vodka, first with tonic then frozen and neat: tipped back in one. By midnight Monk was raging, out of control, but no one wanted to fight him: too big. Boys moved out of reach, allowed girlfriends to flirt with him, defuse, placate: protective role-reversal as old as war itself. He calmed down, apologised, bought drinks all round, introduced them to the first blind man most of them had met, told stories, flashed his cash bigtime. The party lasted till dawn.

It was always the same: the creative genie escaping its bottle to run amok; there was no controlling it, not after a drink or two, not when he was storming. And Monk felt no need to control it; he nurtured it, indulged it. He could almost personify it: a different self, part of his whole but whole of itself, one that demanded absolute freedom, knew no authority, no arbitrary moral codes, whose only truth was its own unbridled pleasure, and whose greatest pleasure was to test the limits.

It would get him killed in the end, nearly had done a thousand times before.

'Sometimes,' he said to the room, 'I just need something to remind me that I'm still alive.'

He opened his eyes, glanced at the clock on the wall behind the bar. There was nothing else for it: he waved the waitress over, ordered coffee, a glass of house red and a plate of pastries: yes, the same kind as he had eaten that morning.

Béatrice brought his wine and coffee and pastries.

'Is Henri here yet?' he asked.

'Upstairs,' she said. 'Getting changed.'

'You can go now if you like. I'll hold the fort.'

He was in charge. His godson Xavier Janssen was away for a week or two, in New York to see his sister Francine. Monk did not mind. The Republic ran itself and being in charge just meant relaxing Xavier's rules for a while.

'You upset Alain.'

'*Oui*. He's only a poet.' Monk pointed at the sign below the clock on the wall behind the bar: No Poets.

'Still.'

'If he scratches so much as a doggerel he's dog meat. Out on his ear.'

'I feel sorry for him.'

'Save it. He's only a poet.'

'Why did he run away?'

'He'll be back.'

'But why?'

'It was just something I said. I know how to get his goat.'

'It's cruel.'

'Nous ne sommes pas libres de faire le mal.'

'Pah. You speak French like a *légionnaire*.'

'I've known a *légionnaire* or two in my time.'

'I'll bet. *Et ce soir?*'

'Oui, ça va?'

'Oui.'

He watched her go, hips swinging, spring in her step. For the hundredth time that week he frowned, tried to find what it was in her that reminded him of Miriam Janssen. Something in her bones, but her posture, too, the way she carried herself, the quiet reserves of desire deep within her.

'Le charme de la mort n'existe que pour les courageux,' he said to the empty room.

He glanced once more at the clock: five minutes past five. Henri was late again, the second day in a row. If Xavier were here, he would fire him.

He gazed blankly at paintings, wished for the hundredth time that week that he had some image of Miriam Janssen: a sketch, a photo, anything that would allow him to see her, imagine her in any way. His mind was empty, his eidetic memory for faces and images useless to him where it had never failed him before.

'*Cache-toi, guerre,*' he whispered to the room.

It was she who had taught him French. Caliban-like he had found his own use for the language.

She had always been there. Lars Janssen had known her since childhood when they would play together in the gardens of Olaf Janssen's villa in Tangiers, she the daughter of Olaf's *colon* housekeeper and an unnamed, unknown Arab: beautiful bastard child. Olaf didn't give a damn about race or class. He became her godfather – did that make her Monk's godsister? Irrelevant: when Miriam and Lars were married, the first time by Buck Rogers in a force-niner off the Azores, Monk as best man, she became more than a sister to him.

He had met her in nineteen-fifty-eight. Eleven years old, jokes at school about Tangiers and little boys: he had not, frankly, understood them: a sheltered lad in many ways; the blast of heat on their arrival, his first trip away from England: eleven years of summers in Cornwall blown to fuck in an explosion of spice and colour and strangely-accented noise.

Early morning after a lonely evening, Lars closeted with Pater until the small hours: the sound of a girl singing in French, glimpses of dark hair bobbing among the shrubs, a flash of hands and feet: cartwheels. It was not until evening that he saw her face: brown eyes, wide smiling mouth, her father's nose calmed by her mother's bones, good blood along the line, a prepubescent vision of beauty for all the prepubescent Monk knew what beauty was.

She spoke fluent Arabic, French and Swedish, and not a word of English, the mystique this added as alluring as Lars's native Swedish and perfect French were excruciating. Olaf: 'I never think she need it, but of course she do. I fix it but for now you teach she. Keep on truckin' boys.'

A long hot summer: English, Swedish, Arabic and French lessons, busman's holiday for a schoolboy, but not all work and no play. The seeds were sown. It came down not to looks or personality or even class or wealth, but geography. He was a guest of the Young Master in the Young Master's father's house, and Miriam, ten-year-old child of her country and her status, was politically astute enough to know where to direct her favour.

Had it bothered him then? Not really. He was reassured by Lars's dismissive nice-enough-but-just-a-girl, seduced by the excitement of camel rides, a week on the *Ringhorn*, the black volcanic sands of Lanzarote, exotic food, servants and wine and the irresistible flame of the Mediterranean sun.

Not until later when she had become almost a woman, his desires those of a man, did the pain and the hunger begin; a memory: the early nineteen-sixties, she would sunbathe naked on the bathing platform aft of the *Ringhorn*, they would swim naked together, the three of them: coarse black hair grazing his hip, razor wire as she slithered by.

And Lars: 'You may look, Monk, but you may not touch.'

The sole indictment.

It was here in London that he had seen her last, May nineteen-eighty: a flying visit, a weekend off from war but it would be another busman's holiday, two days sketching men in their balaclavas, hunting down features to betray their anonymity.

They hugged and kissed. She and Lars laughed at the sight of him in a djellaba: three months with the mujahedeen. They seemed well. Motherhood agreed with her and she had not lost her figure or her looks. Xavier and Francine would be starting school in the autumn, boarding in the week and staying with George, Monk's father, at weekends, the school just a ten-minute drive from the village where he lived.

'They'll get a better education from George than they ever will at school,' said Lars.

'You won't miss them?' Monk asked her.

'Of course,' she said. 'But we can make up for it during the holidays. We're touring the islands this summer, all four of us. George might come as well. Won't you join us?'

Amnesia they called it: the islands of the Pacific, Polynesia, Melanesia, Micronesia, Indonesia, uncounted days exploring, drifting, daydreaming, the *Ringhorn* Lars's by now, Olaf dead three years: a freak accident at sea, the details sketchy but heads had rolled and there had been no funeral, a memorial service instead.

'I thought you might have sold her,' Monk said.

'No,' said Lars. 'It's not what he would have wanted. Besides, what would Janssen Shipping be without its flagship?'

'Strictly legit?'

'That would be dull.'

'I'll think about it,' Monk said. 'I'll see.'

He had not gone; they had never reached Amnesia: the *Ringhorn* destroyed in an explosion just a few weeks later, all hands lost.

They ate well that day. A full English breakfast washed down with Earl Grey tea in pint mugs and taken with sugar and milk. They had Welsh rarebit for elevenses and for lunch they ordered faggots and boiled potatoes and peas. In the afternoon they took afternoon tea: crumpets and muffins and scones with clotted cream, then saffron cake and fruit tea loaf with lots of butter. For supper Lars demanded a whole roasted pig between them, no vegetables, no sauce, just a roast suckling pig to eat with their fingers and wash down with dry white wine from Alsace served cold as ice.

Monk glanced again at the clock: it was growing persistent: eight minutes past five. He shifted in his new armchair, rubbed the back of his hand against the warm leather. He closed his eyes, opened them again immediately.

Buck Rogers's armchair had been a great leather armchair, set on a swivel in the middle of the *Ringhorn*'s bridge. It was not an affectation: the *Ringhorn* was his home; he had been a sailor to his bones, thirty years at sea even before Monk had met him. He was blind in one eye. 'Odin', they called him, behind his back they thought, but he knew well enough. No eyepatch for him, but a lazy glass eye with an iris of deepest blue, a perfect handpainted match got in Japan in nineteen-forty-five, that and half-a-dozen tattoos and a dose of Jap clap as he liked to tell.

Rogers was dead now, so many of them were: stupid deaths, pointless. Rogers had got his in a Manila whorehouse in nineteen-seventy-nine. Nothing sinister: a heart-attack: too much fun.

He had shown Monk the sea. Aged fourteen, he and Lars had spent the summer on the *Ringhorn*, a working vacation learning the ropes. They decided to stay on. Neither Olaf Janssen nor George Monk was of a mind to object, but Olaf: 'The sea, she the best lesson a man can get in life, just so long as you leave before she kill you. Remember this: she kill you in the end, and she won't teach you to leave.'

Keep on truckin' boys.

Rogers gave him the crew name 'Short Order', on account of his height, and put him to work in the short-order galley where he learnt to cook breakfasts and hamburgers and chili-dogs and chicken sandwiches and fast food of every type. He learnt to hate the stink of frying pans and grease, learnt to tolerate humidity and heat; Lars had it worse: cabin boy to Rogers himself, an object lesson in management which would serve him well but which, it had seemed to Monk at the time, stamped some of the fire out of him.

That would have been Olaf's plan. By the nineteen-fifties Janssen Shipping was almost legitimate, a vast floating empire on which the sun never set and which Olaf ruled with uneasy contempt for what he had become. He did not need a chip off the old block for a son, needed a manager, a businessman, not a wiseguy to take the helm. So Lars was sent to school in England, lived with the Monks and learnt middle-class English refinement and reserve over his innate Swedish garrulousness. He was never at home with it.

For four years they served on the *Ringhorn*'s crew, sailed the world, learnt to swear and drink and fuck and fight with the best of them. And Monk learnt to paint. Rogers encouraged him: 'You need an interest, Short Order. What's it to be?' His father had taught him the basics years before and now, for two hours a day, every day, while Lars practised his scales on the Steinway in the saloon, Monk practised composition, colour, texture. He had a natural eye for it and an excellent line, a visual mind, could paint people from memory.

He was just fifteen when Rogers took one look at his latest work, an oil portrait of Juliette, the *Ringhorn*'s first officer, as she leant over a deck rail, smoking a cigarette against a backdrop of sea and sky: 'How much do you want for it, Short Order?'

Monk had shaken his head, wanted no money.

'Well, here's a buck from Buck. You can sign it. Your own name.'

Years later Rogers told him why: 'You showed the beauty in her. Most people didn't see it. I saw it; Olaf saw it. You saw it and you caught it. Knew the moment I saw that picture you'd make a life out of it. That's a talent you have.'

It was not that Juliette was ugly, but she had no hair, the result of some childhood illness, and looked alien, cultivated an attitude to match, took Monk's virginity by way of thanks.

But mostly he cooked and swabbed and polished and cooked. The yacht had a proper galley, of course, with a French chef and a full complement of helpers. The short-order galley was for crew, for food on the hoof, for force-niners when the burgers would flip themselves and Monk could amuse himself making art out of the French's and Heinz which splattered the walls.

He became friends with the chef, a murderer who had joined the *Légion* after sticking his boss in the street one night, served his time in Indochina then was found by Rogers in a fleapit strip-joint off the Warmoestraat in Amsterdam: cook-cum-muscle. 'Never saw a knife like that in my life,' Rogers had said.

It was no knife, but castration shears from the beef farm where Marcel had spent his childhood. Rogers had hired him on sight.

Marcel taught them to shoot and to fight – the *Légion*'s own brand of martial art; from Rogers they learnt to navigate and predict the weather and understand currents; Juliette showed them how to strip an engine in near-darkness, fix it and put it back together better than new. From Eladio, who had saved Monk's father's life in Spain, they learnt to make and set explosives, and to booby-trap them too. And from Olaf himself he and Lars learnt how to kill.

Monk's gaze fell on a painting, one of his own, a charcoal and gouache sketch of Lars dressed in a suit of lights, his hair slicked back, a curly pencil-thin moustache drawn over his lip with Miriam's eyeliner, one hand on his hip, a *muleta* and sword in the other, his body skewed in a mock breast pass, the title: *Maestro*. Monk had lengthened his hair and given him dark, flashing eyes in the representation, but otherwise it had been drawn from life.

It was the last time all of them had been together – his father, Olaf, Lars and Miriam, the children. Nineteen-seventy-seven, George Monk's sixtieth birthday. Olaf wanted to buy him a present, a thank-you for nearly forty years as his right-hand man and architect of the Janssen Shipping empire.

Olaf and George had met in nineteen-thirty-nine. George was up late marking papers when Olaf Janssen rapped on the door of his Holland Park home. George opened up to find Olaf waving a revolver at him. He had just shot a policeman and some others were chasing him. Would George hide him for a while? Even if Olaf had not mentioned half-a-dozen names of friends, George would have helped him: war-tested anarchist with no love for the law and a soul which was hungry for adventure, despised the history-teacher existence to which he had been reduced: half his foot blown off in the defence of Madrid: no more war. He took Olaf in, hid him for a week until the fuss died down, then smuggled him to Southampton where Olaf made good his escape.

Olaf repaid his debt. He asked George to run the legitimate side of Janssen Shipping which Olaf had founded in the nineteen-twenties on the back of a lucrative trade in trafficking aquavit into Montana, which state the Janssen family in those days called home. Since then he had played the adventurer, running drugs and guns, people, anything where there was a profit to be turned and excitement to be had. He needed an executive arm.

And George was up to the job. He made the company millions, bought stock for himself, grew rich beyond his wildest dreams. In nineteen-forty-two he married Alice, aristocratic daughter of a War Office honcho. The invitation to join SIS was forthcoming and Monk Sr made a good spook: Janssen Shipping had contacts everywhere and the traffic in information cut both ways: a win-win situation, as Olaf liked to put it.

In nineteen-forty-six Lars and Charles were born within days of each other, and George became godfather to Lars, Olaf to Charles in a private ceremony on the *Ringhorn*, spanking new out of a shipyard in Sweden and herself christened only weeks before. The respective family fortunes were inextricably bound.

By nineteen-seventy-seven Franco was dead. Olaf suggested a trip to Spain. George refused. He would never go back there, not even forty years on. But if Olaf wanted to bring a piece of Spain to him he would be happy enough.

The village where George Monk had gone to live was a typical English village with a village green where cricket was played every Sunday afternoon, a parish church and three pubs and a post office and a village store. George had spent a fortune doing up the Big House on the hill, stocked the mill ponds with expensive carp, hired a maid and gardeners and a chauffeur and a cook, but no butler.

The arrangements were made in secrecy. George did not know why Olaf wanted to build paddocks in the manor house grounds, just let him get on with it, reminded him now and again that the British police still had a warrant for his arrest. 'As if they know what I look like,' Olaf said.

The bulls arrived first, one hundred great black and grey Moreno bulls from a ranch whose animals were avoided by even the most talented matadors for their size and difficulty. They had been brought by freighter to the Thames Estuary, smuggled ashore and loaded on to flat-bedded trucks and driven the hundred miles to the village, where they were unloaded in the dead of night: snorting, stamping shadows in the darkness.

The next morning the steers arrived, legally imported three months earlier. Then the carpenters came, and the wood. The bullring was to be built on the village green – first the stands, then the fences, then the corrals and finally further fences to line the village streets all the way up to the paddocks in the gardens of Big House. When the bullring was ready the sand came, Albero sand from Andalucia, driven all the way by fat lorry drivers who would stay for the fiesta and were already in the party mood. They filled the night with song and laughter, kissed the girls and made them cry.

The bullfights were to be formally correct. Each day for a week some steers and six bulls chosen by the bulls' breeder would be driven through the streets to the bullring. People could run before them if they wished. At one o'clock lots would be drawn to see which matador would fight which bulls, and at three the fights would commence. Olaf had hired six of the most popular matadors in Spain to kill the animals.

From Jerez came butchers and vintners and chefs and every kind of Spanish speciality: Serrano hams and casks of sherry, olives. From Malaga Olaf had hired a pasodobles band and from Granada flamenco dancers and gypsy musicians. And there would be guests: politicians and businessmen of course, but ordinary people too, working Spaniards whom Olaf was paying simply to be themselves, add colour and life. They worried that it would rain or that it would be windy. It did not rain, the air was still. It was as if God Himself were in Olaf's pocket, for a time, for a price.

'*Dès que l'aurore a paru, les jeunes filles vont cueillir des roses,*' Monk murmured to the room.

A sudden gust of wind blew rose petals in through the open window. There was the sound of a girl laughing on the street below.

He brushed morning dew from the shoulders of his jacket.

Henri arrived at nine minutes past five and Pete Dixon arrived a minute later. Monk ordered a bottle of champagne and some more pastries. Then he told Henri to pour him a glass of apricot schnapps.

'You be careful, Charlie,' Pete Dixon said. 'You drink too much of that stuff and you'll go blind. Then where would you be.'

When Henri had brought their drinks Pete Dixon lit a cigarette and sipped his wine.

'So, Charlie,' he said. 'What's this I hear about you harassing some poor young waitress here? What is this?'

Monk had told Simon Morton about it when he saw him, and by now all the Blind Men would know: the grapevine *par excellence*.

'It's nothing,' said Monk. 'Not really. We went to an opening at a gallery in Clerkenwell. We ate together afterwards. She's nice.'

'This is the French, am I right?'

'They're all French.'

'Béatrice, am I right? Dark, red-brown hair, quite long and in a French style, arranged around her ears, loose down her back; a pretty face and nice eyes: brown with green flecks. Is that the one, Charlie? Am I right?'

'You're right, Pete. Béatrice.'

'Very nice too. I have a little soft spot for her myself.

Don't worry though, I'll stand aside. I'll give you a clear run. When are you seeing her next?'

'Tonight.'

'After the chess?'

Thursday night: chess night in the Exchequer Room; the heady carnivorous rush of the ten-minute games for which the Republic was famous, the breathless hush punctuated only by the clickclack of the clocks, whispered side bets: high-rollers with money to burn. Monk did not play, but he understood the game, the dynamics, the people. Pete Dixon would play: fast chess specialist, hustler to his bones.

'After the chess.'

'And what?'

'A meal somewhere. We'll eat oysters and drink champagne.'

'And then back to your pad and. Are we gonna hustle the Turk tonight? Is he where we want him?'

'Not yet. Another week at least.'

'I'm disappointed. I hate to throw games, but you're the boss. But now you shut up and let me practise.'

Pete Dixon closed his eyes to practise, his lips moving silently as he recited the openings and their variations he had learnt from his talking computer during the previous week: the fine art of losing well.

Monk rubbed his jaw, took a sip of schnapps and a bite of pastry. He brushed crumbs from his lap, watched idly as they jumped up and down on the floorboards and screamed with delight: Again! Again! then disappeared in tiny puffs of smoke.

God moves in mysterious ways, Monk thought to himself.

The poet came back and sat down. He had put pink plastic earplugs in his ears and looked pleased with himself. Monk smiled. Henri caught his eye and tapped his forehead. Monk shrugged. The earplug in the poet's right ear turned to bubblegum, ballooned and popped, chewed itself back into shape. The smell of candy drifted across the room.

'What's that aroma?' Pete Dixon asked.

He ignored the clock, a gooey unreadable mess now in any case. He asked Henri for the time. Quarter past five. He took a sip of schnapps. He looked around the room. He inventoried the paintings. It was time to plan some changes, usher in the autumn. Down with the Hockneys and Warhols, up the Dixes, the Schieles, the Bacons and the Freuds. Art as wallpaper.

'*Le jugement est infaillible,*' he said quietly to himself.

Pete Dixon had fallen asleep.

Monk looked around the room. The Exchequer Room was starting to fill up: the usual mix of journalists and publishers and creative types lured to the place by its atmosphere of millennial decadence and by the golden aura of the Janssen clan. He knew some of them, they all knew him, nodded curtly to him as they caught his eye.

It was then that he saw the woman.

She was standing alone at the bar when suddenly she laughed: an extraordinary, throaty, abandoned laugh which made Monk laugh, sending bubbles up his nose and champagne dripping from his chin.

He knew instantly who she was. She had aged badly: sun, cigarettes, the weight of her grief. But her looks were distinctive. He recognised the clothes. He had known that she would come.

She stared at him for a long moment before walking over catwalk style, soles of her feet slapping gently on the wooden floor, pelvis thrust forward, arms swinging languidly, eyes holding his, her face turned forty degrees to the right. The entire room watched, taking in her dyed-black hair and deeply wrinkled skin, the trousers and brogues, the old tailcoat several sizes too large and threadbare in places, no shirt or blouse underneath, just a black brassière, black gloves: Morticia Addams to a T.

'Well, well, well,' she said. 'If it isn't Charlie Monk.'

She held out her hand for him to shake.

'Galatea. Gala if you prefer.'

Monk motioned for her to sit, called for a glass, poured her champagne.

'Just to take the edge off the day, huh?' she said, ironic, her voice bare feet on pebbles at the beach.

She did not touch the drink, just sat there in silence watching him drink, then: 'You drink champagne like a champagne-drinking fish, Charlie Monk. I should know. We had a fish once, Jean-Louis and Kurt and I, and it did drink champagne, a few drops a day in its bowl. It died from cirrhosis of the liver. Poor thing.'

Monk asked her if the fish got drunk.

'How the hell should I know. It was only a fish. I'll see you tomorrow, Charlie Monk. Same time, same place. I have something for you.'

Then she stood and, with that same bizarre gait, she was gone.

TWO

A PORTRAIT OF THE ARTIST AS A TOTAL ARTIST

1980. Oil on canvas. 134.5 × 112 cm. Self-portrait, drunk, nude and smeared with oil paints. Tate Gallery, London.

NOTES: Painted soon after the death of Lars and Miriam Janssen when their yacht, the *Ringhorn*, sank off Cartagena in Spain, this is among the most personal works of Monk's *oeuvre* and is not generally recognised as a work of war art despite the artist's own assertion that it should be. The cartoon-like qualities of the representation set it apart from Monk's usual rigorous realism and reflect his acknowledged view that his relationship with the Janssen dynasty through three generations imparted a fantasy-esque quality to his life. For most of his career Monk had a Janssen Shipping private jet at his personal disposal and would frequently commute back and forth between war zones – '. . . sipping champagne as I went. It was obscene, but how better to appreciate the obscenity of war than to indulge in the obscenity of wealth even as war rages?' After the Janssens' deaths, Monk entered a prolonged depression of which he never spoke. He is believed to have travelled extensively in Africa during the period, but there is no record of his completing any paintings in that time.

Claude Tartaro, Page 137.

In his room at the Savoy Hotel on the Strand in central London, Claude Tartaro lay on the bed and listened carefully for any sound of the return of the woman who sometimes called herself Galatea or Gala but whose real name was Grace Matthews and whose room adjoined his own. She had left an hour earlier, perhaps more than an hour. His sense of time had been taken from him along with his eyesight, a curious, dislocating side effect. There was a clock in the room. It ticktocked tauntingly.

Doubts nagged at him as they had ever since they left Spain. Was it her plan to abandon him here? The punishment she had devised for him two years earlier was subtle and exact and he rarely knew what she might do next.

He opened his eyes, flinched as he always did. Two years had been enough to learn the simple tasks he needed in order to subsist in Grace Matthews's grandiose fantasy world, but he doubted if a lifetime would prepare him for the shock of opening his eyes to discover darkness where he knew there should be light. He closed his eyes again.

He had no regrets.

The Image was imprinted on his mind. It had been the last thing he saw with any clarity and it was as if, by then taking away his sight, Grace Matthews had unwittingly helped to preserve his memory. There was nothing super-imposed, nothing to refract or diffract his recollection of every detail of Miriam Janssen's face and body. It seemed to Tartaro that Grace Matthews had not simply helped to preserve this memory, but had intensified it. It was not what she would have intended.

It began in nineteen-sixty-seven.

Tartaro arrived by train from his home village in the Pyrenees. He should have been nervous, but his father's Spanish machismo had formed him every bit as much as his mother's French sensitivity and thirst for knowledge. Despite being from the provinces, Tartaro considered himself to be a rounded individual, a sophisticate for whom a degree course at the Sorbonne was more rite of passage or formal initiation than essential element in his education or upbringing. He had come to Paris to begin his life. He would seek a career in the arts, probably as a writer and critic. He would find himself a beautiful and wealthy wife, make a beautiful home with beautiful children, live a beautiful existence.

He was not the only one in their class to fall in love with her. He supposed they all did. His arrogance was his downfall. They all knew she was married, that her husband was sole scion of one of the wealthiest families on earth, that her father-in-law was a gangster who lived above the law to the extent that it was said that even MI6 and the CIA were in his pocket. Where the others were content to admire from afar or befriend her in platonic manner, Tartaro was single-minded in his pursuit of her. He knew that no material items would seduce her, no psychology would dissolve the immanence of her self-knowledge and confidence. Rather he placed his trust in a characteristic he ascribed to all women: the endlessness of their longing. Tartaro concluded that by testing the limits of her imagination he might discover her hidden desires and, in so doing, break a path to her heart.

He pressed on her the works of de Sade, Sacher Masoch and Lautréamont, discussed with her Pauline Réage and his own theory that *The Story of O* was a brilliant feminist tract from an existentialist model. She seemed receptive to his ideas, would invite him unprompted to join her in her apartment on the Left Bank where they would sit and talk until the early hours. Every day he fell further in love with her and every day, without changing in any way, she grew more remote from him.

He became more direct, invited her to experiment with domination, either as mistress or as slave. It did not need to be sexual, he said, but an intellectual exercise in control and obedience. She declined. He suggested that they spend time together naked in an effort to remove the sexual tension he felt in their relationship. By growing accustomed to her nudity, he suggested, he would gradually eliminate his sexual desire for her. She declined.

'In my experience, spending time naked with others only increases sexual desire. I'm a married woman,' she said. 'I won't do that any more.'

Tartaro felt a jarring jealousy. There were other men who had seen her body.

Finally he overstepped the mark.

It was May nineteen-sixty-eight. He took no part in the

protests, approved of them in theory but despised the crowd mentality which accompanied them as students who had never before thought of more than their next beer painted slogans on walls and burnt cars. He invited her to leave the city for a few days, to travel with him to his parents' village until the crisis was over. She declined. A childhood friend who was now a very talented artist was travelling to Paris to paint her portrait. The arrangement was long-standing and Charles Monk was not the kind of man who would fear the turmoil of the *événements*.

'He'll feel right at home,' she said.

At first Tartaro felt only a mild curiosity, but when she told him that the portrait was to be a full-length nude he knew with unfailing certainty that if he could not see her in the flesh, he must see the painting.

'It's out of the question.'

'But why? You pose for this artist, what's the point if no one will see it?'

'Lars will see it. I am doing it for Lars. And I'm only doing it on condition that no one but Lars sees it. And Charlie, of course. When it's finished it will be taken to the boat and hung in our stateroom where no one else is allowed to go, and that will be an end to it.'

'I don't understand your attitude.'

'You don't need to understand it. You just have to accept it.'

The next day Tartaro went to the library to discover everything he could about Charles Monk. The information was sketchy, but he unearthed a photograph of a bear of a man with the face of a grotesque, the caved-in features of a Marseille hood, a skewed nose and the appearance of a person whose left side was paralysed. He would discover later that it was only Monk's face that was paralysed, that tears wept constantly from his left eye, mucus dripping from his nose, saliva collecting in the corner of his mouth. In every way he presented a disgusting figure.

And yet he was a talented artist, Tartaro could not deny it. An artist with the ability to capture the essence of his subjects. One painting in particular struck him. Done in nineteen-sixty-six, it was a portrait of an elderly Vietnamese woman with her head partly bowed, her face painted as a death mask. Later, Monk would tell him that the work was provoked by the death of a young Vietnamese girl in a grenade attack on a Saigon café where Monk was sitting at the time. Monk was injured in the attack when a fragment of one of the girl's bones lodged in his thigh. The girl's body was effectively destroyed but, Monk said, her head remained entirely intact, just a comical smudge of dust dabbed on the end of its nose. The disembodied head was cradled for a long time by the woman portrayed in the painting.

It seemed to Tartaro that the old woman's tears, filling and magnifying the deep wrinkles in her skin, trapped the sunlight and gave the illusion that the death mask was encrusted with jewels. It was as if, by portraying the woman in the banal terms of an *objet d'art*, the artist had highlighted the permanence of human beauty in the face of suffering. Tartaro was touched despite himself.

Monk would arrive that day. He had an appointment in the afternoon but would see Miriam in the evening. Tartaro resolved to see her first, to allay her fears about him and inveigle his way into a meeting with Monk.

'He loves to meet anyone,' she said. 'Just don't ask him about the painting. He never talks about his works in progress. I'll get you round one evening,' she said.

It was not until mid-June that she invited him to a meal at her apartment.

Monk was there, some students Tartaro had met before, a minor philosopher of whom he had heard, a poet who was known for plagiarism of ideas if not words. She sat him next to Monk's own guest, an eighteen-year-old female *novillero* from Spain who had recently been gored in the stomach and was convalescing at Monk's expense in a private clinic in the suburbs.

They were instantly distrustful of one another. In Tartaro's mind Monk was nothing less than a fascist with a fascist girlfriend to boot. The man spent the evening railing against the students: 'Whores for idiocy, every one of them'; defending bullfighting: 'Morally indefensible, but only if you accept a morality which takes a hatchet to beauty'; playing the apologist for American intervention in Vietnam: 'Communists are scum'; and arguing in favour of appeasement in World War Two: 'They would have deported the Jews instead of killing them and thirty million lives wouldn't have been needlessly lost in a war of absurd principle. History would have got rid of Hitler without any help from the rest of us.'

Yet even as he thought to despise Monk's arguments and to refute them, Tartaro knew deep inside himself that these were his own views, the views he would never have the courage to express openly in the current climate. He wished to dislike Monk, but found in him a kindred spirit, and fancied that although Monk was at his most scathing when rebutting Tartaro's arguments, he reserved a degree of respect for him that was absent in his dealings with the others at the table.

He studied Monk's face, the crusted yellow trails of evaporated fluids, the damaged bones, the scars on ears and cheeks and lips, the angry furrows in his forehead; finally his eyes. But Tartaro could not look there. When Monk caught his eye he felt suddenly assaulted, as if his soul were being invaded, captured by some alien entity. He closed his eyes briefly, opened them again.

By the end of the evening the two of them were at the dining table alone, the others next door endlessly agreeing with one another while Tartaro and Monk sparred.

Finally Monk seemed to tire of the cut and thrust and rested back in his chair, lit a huge Cuban cigar and bellowed to Miriam for more coffee and a glass of port which she brought to him with a kiss on the cheek.

'I admire your work,' Tartaro told him, diffidently.

'I'm learning. Some is good, some not. It's a question of discovering what to discard.'

'Hemingway said that every great writer needs a built-in shit-detector. I suppose it must be the same for artists.'

'I suppose, but I would be lying if I said it was built in from birth. For me it comes with learning what I like to look at and understanding the difference between what I like and what is actually beautiful. It only comes with practice.'

Tartaro was taken aback. It seemed inconceivable to him that a fellow aesthete should confess such a weakness.

'You doubt your own taste?' he asked, the surprise clear in his voice.

Monk smiled genially, sipped his port, puffed on his cigar. Tartaro understood instantly that he had sprung a carefully laid trap. He prepared himself for the *coup de grâce*.

'We're the same age, you and I.'

Again Tartaro was ambushed, this time by the gentleness in Monk's tone.

'Give or take a year. Your point?'

'We're both still young. There was a time when I had no doubts about my own taste. When I thought I knew what beauty was. And some things I once thought beautiful I still find beautiful. The bullfight, for example, has lost none of its beauty for me. Or the paintings of Schiele or the music of Orff or the poetry of Rilke or the novels of Camus. But these are all artists who have at least looked for a place beyond morality, have understood in some way that beauty continues to exist in the absence of morality, that while our appreciation of beauty might be influenced by our moral codes, beauty itself disdains morality, has no interest in it, no need for it. It is only we who need to be either good or bad.

'I've already seen more than I need to. I've seen young girls blown to pieces by explosives which had been strapped to their bodies by people who had children of their own, children they loved as you or I would love our own children. I've seen men cut off other men's cocks and balls and then stuff them in their mouths to stop the screaming. I've seen middle-class white American college kids take it in turns to rape an eighty-year-old grand-

mother because they wanted to know what it would be like
to get head from a woman who had no teeth—'

'You stood by and watched?'

'You think I would be here now if I hadn't? But please,
these are everyday events in the places I have been to, not
exceptions. I have few opinions on the rights or wrongs of
any war, but I do know that war is a place where moral
codes are altered, inverted. The ideal place to look for
beauty if you're weighed down with the baggage of good
and evil.'

Monk waved a hand in the direction of the street.

'Them, out there, if I showed them a portrait of a naked
American soldier, all muscle and cock, they'd call it fascist
art, a celebration of Yankee imperialism, they'd call me
names. They'd forget that it was simply a portrait of a
physically near-perfect human male who just happened to
be killing women and children for a living. They'd
superimpose their moral view and never see the beauty. I'm
not immune to that. I have moral codes and just because I
know they're arbitrary doesn't stop even the language I
speak from reinforcing them at every turn. Yes, I doubt my
taste. I doubt my ability to see beauty. I doubt my ability
at any given time to see beyond what I think is right or
wrong. I've learnt the lesson more quickly, at a younger
age than I might have liked. It was forced upon me. But I
think it's a lesson we all learn. Sooner or later.'

'But there must be some moral dimension to your art,
surely?'

'There are many. There are those which have crept in
unnoticed by myself – the arbitrary codes, the false codes.
And there are those moral dimensions which are bound to

beauty itself. Don't misunderstand me, Monsieur Tartaro. I'm all in favour of the idea of an honest moral code. I believe such a code may well exist and that it may resemble some of the codes we already elect to follow – or disregard – but it's a code which can be validated by the truth, by beauty, by science. Not by God or bleeding hearts or even by radical subjectivity.'

Tartaro snorted.

'You'd have a moral code based on mathematics? It has been done before, Mr Monk. Herr Leibniz's approach was generally judged to be a failure.'

'What is pi-r-squared?' Monk asked abruptly.

'The area of a circle, of course.'

'But a circle is its area. So in mathematical terms, if we know pi and r and the meaning of squared, we can say that pi-r-squared is the circle – the Platonic ideal of the circle, if you will. You concede?'

'Again, your point?'

'We live in a universe of shapes, patterns. Theoretically every one of them can be described in mathematical terms, in terms of numbers relative to one another. Beauty itself is form, shape, pattern. I contend, Monsieur Tartaro, that any beautiful thing must have a mathematical description waiting to be defined and, further, that if the mathematical descriptions of a great many beautiful forms were to be uncovered, a fundamental constant would be found to apply – a function of beauty, if you will. Is it not then possible, since our appreciation of beauty is coloured by our moral standpoint, that by defining beauty in scientific terms we might learn which moral standpoint most accurately identifies beauty? In doing so, would we not have uncovered a moral code which, if not quite based on mathematics, could at least be justified by mathematics, by science?'

'You could end up with the morality of Hitler. Would you wish that on us?'

'The Nazis were not noted for the quality of their aesthetic judgement, Monsieur Tartaro. I agree, however, that a morality discovered in this way would be a violent one at times. The morality of the Greek gods, perhaps. The morality of Pallas Athene who flayed her enemies and wore their skins, the virgin goddess of storms and of battle and of plunder, the goddess who devised the Trojan Horse and set the head of Medusa at the centre of her goatskin shield, who was protector to Hercules and Perseus and Theseus and the Argonauts. And yet in peacetime she was Athene, the goddess of the arts, of healing, of all kinds of crafts – inventor of the flute, the plough, the loom, creator of the olive tree. Did you know that if you wish to make an offering to Pallas Athene you must sacrifice a goat? A morality bound to the sacrifice of goats would be a fine thing, Monsieur Tartaro. Do you not agree?'

Confused, Tartaro had no reply.

He did not have the courage to ask if he might view the painting when it was complete. There was something in Monk's strange zeal which persuaded him that even to ask would be dangerous. Instead, Tartaro decided that he would break into the studio Monk had rented close to Miriam's apartment. He did not know where to begin, and knew no one who would help him, but he had to see the painting, he had to see what Monk saw.

She told him it was complete.

'The day after tomorrow I'll fly with Charlie to London. We'll unveil it to Lars.'

'And how does it look?'

'I don't know. I haven't seen it yet. He'll show me it tomorrow. I'll insist!'

They were in a café near his apartment by the Gard du Nord. He already knew that she had keys to Monk's studio. She had let it slip after Monk had disappeared for a few days, a side trip to America where he had painted the dead Robert Kennedy as a favour for Miriam's father-in-law.

She went to the toilet. He stole her keys.

They were waiting for him.

'You must think I'm a fool, Claude. You really imagine that I would lose my keys like that?'

Monk was sitting in an armchair, the painting beside him covered with a dust-sheet. He was smoking a cigar and wearing sunglasses although it was after midnight. He did not say a word.

'Go!' she said. 'I never want to see you again.'

THREE

You Sometimes Get a Fuck, But You Always Get Fucked

1976. Oil on canvas. 112.3 × 95.3 cm. Portrait of young black woman, South Africa. Republic, London.

NOTES: Title is from Raoul Vaneigem. Monk was an avid proponent of Vaneigem's theory of 'radical subjectivity', though he was never a member of the SI, having been barred from entry by Guy Debord. The picture is of Freedom Chance (probably a pseudonym), a young woman who, very publicly, became Monk's lover during the Soweto riots. The relationship encouraged a small number of white liberals in South Africa to engage in sexual relations with black pro-testers as a political statement against apartheid, something which appalled Monk who described protesters and liberals alike as 'whores for idiocy' on the occasion of the work's unveiling in Tangiers. Few details of Monk's relationship with Chance are available, but the couple are believed to have separated early in nineteen-seventy-seven, circumstantial evidence suggesting that Chance bore a child by the artist.

Claude Tartaro, Page 134.

Charles Monk lay on the bed in his penthouse studio in the Janssen-owned hotel next door to the Republic on Russia Street in west London with his eyes wide open. Beside him, Béatrice slept fitfully. It was hot, the heat was oppressive, he was hungry. He could not sleep.

He got up and went through to the kitchenette attached to the studio. He opened the fridge. It was well-stocked as always with cold cuts and cheeses and pickles. On the counter was a fresh loaf of bread left by the maid that afternoon. He tore some bread from the loaf and cut some cheese, skewered a pickle and some meat. As he ate he stood in the doorway and watched Béatrice sleep.

He did not know where it had come from. She was half his age, an aspiring screenplay writer, a Republic regular. Working there allowed her to mingle with the right people at the right price – *nada*, and drinks on the house. It was her idea to go out for an evening. She expressed an interest in the Republic's art collection, suggested a visit to a gallery. There was an opening at a studio in Clerkenwell: 'You can buy me dinner afterwards,' she said.

She spent two hours over pasta and wine talking about films. They did not talk about art – his or anyone else's. The works at the opening had been piss and shit, but Monk held his tongue. The artists were her friends.

The morning after, he woke to a feeling of intense pain,

as if his eyeballs had been sucked dry of their vitreous humour. Fuck, he thought. I'm in love.

He did not know where it had come from. She was an attractive enough girl, but Monk had known many women a dozen times as beautiful. She had an infectious laugh, and she did make him feel young again, the way she persuaded a boy on the Tube to give up his seat by telling him that 'her father' was terminally ill with an unknown condition, too weak to stand and sway.

He was not in love.

Under his breath he said to the room: '*Si la morale de Cléopatre eût été moins courte, la face de la terre aurait changé. Son nez n'en serait devenu plus long.*'

He had a sudden fleeting vision of Miriam Janssen wearing a dressing gown – his dressing gown – coming up behind him as he sits in his studio drinking coffee and smoking a cigarette, hugging him around the neck. He turns: sleepyhead but bright-eyed in the morning light, happy, warm with the remnants of night clinging to her, the day yet to take its toll.

Strange. He had not smoked a cigarette in years.

He lay down beside Béatrice, jogged her arm as he did so. She stirred and opened her eyes.

'*Ça va?*' he asked.

'*Oui, ça va,*' she said. 'My feet hurt.'

He caressed her feet.

'How long have I slept?' she asked.

'Ten, fifteen minutes.'

'Good.'

She looked at him and pursed her lips slightly, avoided his eyes.

'Would it be better if I loved you?' he asked her.

'*Non.*'

'Worse?'

'Perhaps.'

He held her foot against his cheek.

'I'm gentle,' he said.

'With your hands, not with your soul.'

'I'm sorry.'

'At least you have a soul.'

He brushed his lips against her right ear.

'You see?'

'No.'

'This tenderness, but you don't love me. It's insufferable.'

'*L'amour n'est pas le bonheur.*'

She shook him off, sat up, lit a cigarette. She looked at her watch.

'Give me some wine,' she said. 'There's some left?'

'There's some left. But you drink too much.'

'Your sense of humour is very tiring.'

'Then we should sleep.'

'This is English humour, *non*? Very tiring indeed. But I don't want to sleep. I want to sit and drink and smoke and talk and then I want, well, we'll see what I want when I want it. You want some wine?'

'Yes.'

'How is it, *la faim*?'

'It's OK now. It's there, but it's better.'

'I would like to be painted by you, Charlie.'

'It's too late for that. I could sketch you perhaps. An essay.'

'I would like it. To have you admire me for some time. It would be erotic, I think.'

'Yes.'

'Do you get aroused when you paint a woman?'

'Sometimes.'

'I would find that very flattering.'

'But it's deceptive. It's the act of painting that arouses me. Not the act of looking.'

'You're going to tell me some shit now about making love to the canvas, but I will laugh at you if you do.'

'No, I won't tell you that. But only because you would laugh at me.'

She laughed at him.

'Humility is a valuable quality for any artist to possess,' he said.

They were quiet for a while, smoked, drank.

'I knew an artist once,' he said. 'In Vietnam. A monk who did not consider a work complete unless he had ejaculated on to it and mixed his semen with the paint.'

'That's disgusting.'

'But probably commonplace.'

'You do not do this.'

'No. But I understand it.'

'It's disgusting.'

'He's dead now, but he was an interesting man. He was obsessed with the sun, with the fact that all of us and everything on earth come from the same thing as the sun is made of. He ruined his eyes by staring at it.'

'Every fool knows you should not stare at the sun.'

'He was obsessed with it. He couldn't help himself. It was his obsession. We paint with sunlight on sunlight, he would say. In scientific terms I suppose he might have been right.'

'Did he go blind?'

'No, but it reached a point where he could only see things on the periphery of his vision. He killed himself in protest at the war. I watched him do it. I painted him doing it.'

'He allowed this?'

'He encouraged it.'

'You have many blind friends.'

'It was an accident. It seemed like a good idea at the time.'

'Do you regret it?'

'They will have a new member tomorrow – no, today. He's coming to the club. Tartaro. He's called Claude Tartaro.'

'What about him?'

Monk shrugged. 'His eyes were put out with acid.'

'I don't believe you.'

'It's true, and by a man I once knew.'

'Well, I hope he's in prison now, this man you once knew.'

'*Non.* He's the kind of man who does not go to prison.'

'And why did he do it?'

'Tartaro must have offended him in some way.' Monk shrugged.

'But you don't know.'

'No. I don't know.'

'Or perhaps you do. It doesn't matter. You don't have

to tell me. And how do you know this man, this gangster?'

'He was an associate of my godfather. Xavier's grandfather.'

'I should not be surprised. Xavier is like a *mafioso*, but really.'

'Yes. He's a chip off the old block.'

'It doesn't make sense.'

'It doesn't have to. I need a cigar.'

'And another bottle of wine. There is some?'

'Of course.'

Monk got out of bed and went through to the kitchenette, fetched a cigar and a bottle of wine, opened the bottle and went back through to the studio. He paused at the door and studied her, the definition of the muscles in her back.

'Don't stare at me like that,' she said.

'You said you wanted to be admired.'

'But not like that. Give me some.'

He filled her glass then his own, clipped his cigar and lit it. She waved smoke away, lit a new cigarette from the old.

'When the bulls were killed they were butchered and roasted while their flesh was still warm,' he said.

'Who got their balls?'

'Those we ate sliced and fried, on buttered toast.'

'I would like to eat sliced and fried bull's balls on buttered toast. Did you love your father?'

'I was a bad son, but yes.'

'Was he a good father?'

'He was an anarchist. He let me do what I wanted. For me it was good. He was a spy, as well.'

'I don't believe you.'

'*C'est vrai*. It was ironic. Olaf was rich before the war, but it was my father who made him so rich.'

'And your father? Did he become rich?'

'Yes. He was *consigliere*.'

'And you?'

'Now I am *consigliere*.'

'You are *mafioso*.'

'No. Everything is legal now.'

'So why does he need a *consigliere*?'

'He needs someone who understands how it was in the old days.'

'Just in case.'

'Just in case.'

'Just in case. Do you know if he is an attractive man? This new blind man, this Tartaro. Have you met him?'

'I've never met him. His name rings a bell. I don't know what he looks like. We'll see. He'll come in the afternoon, I don't know exactly when. I'm told that he collects birds.'

'I don't like birds.'

'He does. He has dozens of them.'

'I don't like birds. Touch me.'

'Where?'

'Anywhere. Just touch me.'

He stroked her arm with the back of his hand.

'What is his name? The *mafioso*.'

'William Matthews. Sweet William, they call him, or Stinking Billy, or sometimes just the Surgeon.'

'He's a doctor?'

'No. He was once a locksmith, the son and grandson of locksmiths and locksmiths' sons and grandsons. Before he was fifteen years old he could open any lock in the world within minutes of being handed it. He was an artist with the paperclip and penknife. It drove him mad. There was no secret safe from him, but he was haunted by the fact that no secret of his could be secured by any mere lock, that there were others as talented with the penknife and paperclip as he. So he found better ways to secure his secrets. And those of my godfather and his family, my family. And of others. For a long time I made myself forget him, forget his very existence.'

He shrugged. 'Do you find that? People leave your life and you expect never to see them again and suddenly, one day, there they are.'

'Do you always fuck the women you paint?'

'No.'

'But often?'

'Yes. Afterwards.'

'It must be like rape.'

'It is rape. Every time.'

'I heard of a woman, a farmer's wife in the Camargue I think it was, who liked to eat raw liver, still warm, straight from the animal.'

'We did this too.'

'And?'

'When you bite my skin don't you sometimes want to chew clean through?'

'Of course.'

'Perhaps I'll take you to Spain.'

She shook her head slowly. A single tear trickled down her cheek. He caressed her cheek.

'You talk so much shit,' she said. 'Give me more wine.'

'You're drinking too fast.'

He poured her some more wine. She took a large gulp. It was getting light.

'It's getting light,' he said.

'*Oui. Encore une fois, hein?*'

'*J'ai faim.*'

She rubbed his stomach. 'Can you never lie to me?'

'No.'

He rolled off the bed. On the table in the middle of the room there was a bowl of apples. He took an apple, bit into it, chewed slowly, swallowed.

'You destroy your subject.'

'I can buy more in the morning, later. It's not important.'

'They won't be the same, the colours, the shapes, the sizes. They won't be the same.'

'It was just an essay. It's not important.'

Monk took another bite of the apple, then another.

'Or perhaps you could put the core back in the bowl. That would be very semiological.'

'I eat the core. Pips and all.'

'It can't be good for you to eat the core. It must be bad for the stomach.'

Monk threw the apple core through the open studio window.

'I have a picture in my mind of them playing cricket on the bloodstained sand.'

'They took it away, the sand. I don't know where they took it.'

'You are prosaic.'

'But before they took it away we did play cricket. The day after the fiesta was over. The English against the

Spanish. We cleared a wicket, but the outfield was slow.'

'Did you win?'

'They didn't know the rules.'

'What if it landed on someone?'

'Apple cores from heaven.'

'I think it's sad. We should be able to throw an apple core through the window and twenty years later we should be able to pick fruit from the tree that grows where the apple core landed. The world would be a better place.'

He kissed her on the nose. She wrinkled her nose.

'And in any case, by the time I get to them they will have lost some of their moisture. They will be more ripe, shrunken, different. It was just an essay.'

'Have you ever been in love?'

'Once, with someone who looked a little like you, the same bones at least. She was Xavier and Francine's mother. Miriam.

'It was physically painful for me to look at her. When I painted her I had to not-look at her in order to see her. Those were the most difficult portraits I have ever done. They were always based on glimpses of her, flashes. That's not how I normally work. But to look at her made me feel ill. It was like having a knotted cord threaded from my groin to the nape of my neck, invisible hands sawing it back and forth. I couldn't look at her.'

'So you should have stuck to what you know best. Guns and ammo.'

'You misunderstand. I never painted images of war, not once. I only ever painted faces, sometimes bodies. Of course, they were the faces and bodies of people who had been touched by war, that was the point. But the tools, the weapons of war? Not that.'

'And she? She was touched by war?'

He said nothing for a while. She smoked and drank.

'She was a strong and wise woman. Her gift was the olive branch, not the horse.'

'How did you get this one?'

'When I was a child, playing in the garden. I fell out of a tree.'

He shrugged. She fingered the scar.

'Not a very romantic scar,' she said.

'No.'

'What did she look like?'

'She was beautiful.'

'And you have a painting of her?'

'I don't know where they are. When I was young I made many of her, essays, on the boat. Some were destroyed with it, others were stolen, sold, whatever.'

'You don't care?'

'They weren't important. I only ever painted her properly the one time.'

He shook his head, breathed deeply.

'Again, destroyed. The essays were not important.'

'I bet the collectors would not say so now. Was it a good painting, the proper one you did of her?'

'The best work I have ever done. A dangerous work. Big, life-sized. And if you were in a room with it you would think she was standing there herself. Perhaps it's better that it's gone.'

'You could paint her again? From memory? From photographs?'

'No, there are no photographs, and I don't see her face.'

'But you must. You told me this.'

'It's true. I have a perfect memory for faces, but not hers. I can't see her any more.'

'Then you should have kept the sketches.'

'I have a friend who is a poet, a real poet, not like Alain. He refuses to speak with anyone on the telephone: only ever writes letters to people or meets them in person. He's a well-known poet, and you can say that some of his letters are masterpieces of the letter-writing form, but they're still just letters. Even when he plays with words and the rhythm of the language, practises, it's still just a letter. Some idiot who wants to write a biography of him asked me for copies of every letter he'd ever sent me. When I told him I'd thrown them away he went crazy, shouting and screaming at me about priceless jewels and swine. But they were just letters, not poems, not important. That's how I feel about my sketches. When I can, I destroy them, unless there's a sentimental value for someone else.'

Béatrice rolled off the bed and crossed to a small canvas leaning against the wall.

'And this? This is an essay?'

'After a fashion. The other morning, before breakfast, I soaked some paper and clamped it to the easel, drank a coffee while I waited for the paper to dry. It's a routine. I set out the paints, the palette, the brushes, pull on my smock, bring a jar of water from the kitchen. Well, there was a vase of flowers on the table, where the apples are now, put there by the maid the day before, I don't know what kind, just normal yellow flowers in a glass vase and I thought I might paint them, an essay. Even before I'd finished the first wash the flowers seemed to have grown in luminosity. Their yellowness had intensified. It was as if their features had been drawn into relief by my very act of studying them, their detail showing itself more and more until the notion of painting them, of trying to capture them, seemed arrogant and futile. I put down my brush and sat here on the bed staring at the flowers for half-an-hour. I was enthralled by them. I couldn't move. I couldn't paint.'

'*Et puis?*'

She sat down on the bed again, kissed his neck.

'It made me frustrated. I threw the vase across the room, smashed it against the wall. There was glass and water and yellow petals everywhere. The maid found me on my knees picking up the pieces. My fingers were bloody. I realised that this was the essay. Not the flowers, but the lesson in seeing, the pain caused by not seeing, or by seeing too much. So the blood became my paint and I used it to glue yellow petals and tiny shards of glass to the paper. Of course, now the blood is dried and black and the petals will wither to nothing, and eventually there will only be the glass. But simply because a work is ephemeral doesn't mean it has no value. Just that the value is of a different order. The point is, it shouldn't be pickled or picked over. Leave it be, let it rot, burn it.'

She poked at the picture, sucked blood from her finger.

'I would like to know how she looked. There are really no photos of her?'

'They were very private people. They never allowed their pictures to be taken. It was quite unusual. Two of the wealthiest people on the planet and they could walk the streets of London and not a soul would know who they were.'

'I love to see old photographs from when I was a child.'

'And it is for the children that I wish I could see her. Xavier and Francine don't remember what she looked like, not really.'

'It's a shame. If you have no mother I suppose a picture can be something.'

'You know that the eye is part of the brain? *C'est vrai.* I remember when I first heard this – and the fact that the eye can see a single particle of light. It was as if God had come knocking at my door first thing in the morning after a night before. You open the door and there's God. Your hair's a mess and your breath stinks and you're, "Hello God, come in, take a seat: I'll put the kettle on." It doesn't work, somehow.

'And you know, it's not just that the eye can see a single particle of light, it's that it knows to ignore it. It knows that a single particle of light won't tell it jack shit so it waits until it gets four or five particles of light before it bothers thinking about what it's seeing. That for me is incredible. For any artist it must be, to consider how precise one can be in one's art, and yet how imprecise one's fingers are, one's control of the brush. You can do a good approximation, but up against the perfection of the eye you can never be perfect; against the precision of the eye you have no precision at all.'

'Humility is a valuable quality for any artist to possess,' she said.

'*Touché,*' he said.

He shrugged.

'If you had a photo of her you would be able to see her.'

'*Ne reniez pas l'immortalité de l'âme.*'

'Pah. You speak French like a *légionnaire*.'

'I've known a *légionnaire* or two in my time.'

She smiled. 'Touch me.'

'Where?'

'Anywhere. Just touch me.'

He traced the curves of her left leg, then her right.

'*Je t'aime,*' she said, whispered.

'"I love you"', he said, 'is always followed by a thousand unspoken "buts".'

She hit him, but not hard.

'Give me some more wine,' she said.

Monk poured wine. She got off the bed and walked around the room.

'But this is not an essay,' she said.

'No. Not an essay.'

'What's it called?'

'*On the Importance of Surprise when Attacking the Enemy.*'

'It's the death of Balder, *non*?'

'You know the story?'

'Of course. Balder the beautiful, killed by his blind brother Hod with a dart made of mistletoe. Everyone must know it. And you have made it very semiological. Very semiological indeed.'

'It's true.'

'Some I understand, some not. Why the cross?'

'Because legend has it that mistletoe was once a tree, but that its wood was used to make the cross on which Christ was crucified. The death of Balder was the beginning of Ragnarok, the end of the old gods.'

'Of course. Very semiological indeed.'

'He was my best friend and he was married to the only woman I have ever loved. There were times when I wished him dead. There are times when that is more difficult for me to live with than anything else.'

'Sometimes we get what we wish for.'

'Always, I think.'

'And now? What do you wish for now?'

'I've seen too much. Sometimes, more than anything, I would like not to see.'

'Because you have looked.'

'Of course. We look, we see, we see too much, it haunts us.'

'It doesn't make sense,' she said. 'But I know a man who knew a man who was obsessed with the sun. He ruined his eyes by staring at it.'

Monk smiled. He kissed her shoulder, stroked her back.

'Have you had many lovers?' she asked.

'Hundreds,' he said. 'Perhaps thousands. I don't keep count.'

'Tell me about them.'

'All of them?'

'Who were the most interesting?'

Monk sat up, sipped wine, sighed.

'I remember their faces, nearly every one of them. I could paint them for you now, from memory, capture every line and freckle. There was the American girl, blonde and tall, I was just a kid, so surprised to discover that this woman thought she loved me—'

'That's always a surprise.'

'You're right, but the real surprise was to find that as well as loving me, she feared me – imagine! Another time I loved a girl, but she scared me, the intensity she loved me with, it was too much. Or another time a woman who was so, predatory is the only word, that she gave the illusion of great intelligence. It's true that all predators give the impression of intelligence, but it's only a certain kind of intelligence. It took me months to discover that in every other way she was perhaps the most stupid woman I had ever met in my life. And then there have been those women who have tried to seduce me by exposing themselves to me. An intriguing ploy.'

'Did any of them succeed?'

'Most of them, but no thanks to their methods. Perhaps every woman does it at some point in her life. It has happened to me so many times I assume it must be commonplace.'

'I've never done it, but I suppose it's part of childhood as well.'

'If I show you mine.'

'I knew a girl when I was at school who horrified the whole town by stripping in front of half-a-dozen boys. We were very young, though. She's a famous actress now, in Hollywood, but I heard that in her contracts it says she won't take her clothes off.'

'That makes sense. Or there were the ones who were seduced by the strangest things. I remember one, she was a Mossad agent but an American, this would have been in nineteen-seventy or so, in Saigon. I pursued her for months without success, and in the end what did it was when I took her for a meal at a French place which had been attacked with grenades so many times hardly anyone ever went there any more. It had an old French waiter, I forget his name, but he'd lived in Saigon for decades. His speciality was to scream at anyone who complained about the slightest thing or did anything that didn't conform to his idea of how things should be. I ordered champagne and when it came it was warm. All I did was send it back and ask for a properly chilled bottle and he was fine about it, apologised, gave us the bottle on the house, no one drinks warm champagne after all. But it was enough for her to see me do something that not one other person in Vietnam would have dared to do. We had a good time together but she was killed soon afterwards – a friendly-fire incident, they said, but I never believed that for a minute.'

'Have you ever killed anyone?' she asked.

He said nothing.

'I am not shocked,' she said. 'You don't have to tell me anything.'

'I have seen too much,' he said. 'That's all.'

FOUR

HUNGER AS A MOTIVATING FACTOR IN THE ISSUE OF WAR

1977. Oil on canvas. 92.2 × 78.4 cm. Corpse of emaciated Cambodian baby with muzzle of dog investigating. Metropolitan Museum, New York.

NOTES: The symbolism of a dog probing a baby's corpse was lost on most contemporary critics. Dog is eaten in several South East Asian countries, including Cambodia, and the intended implication of a dog assessing the edibility of a dead human baby makes this among the bleakest of Monk's works of the period.

Claude Tartaro, Page 123.

Tartaro had not slept. It was morning, he could tell. The noise of the city waking penetrated even these walls. There was no sound from Grace Matthews's suite. She and her husband had been drunk by the time they returned the night before. They had not checked on him. They had tired of him. They no longer found satisfaction in his suffering, perhaps sensed that their torture was hollow, meant more to them than it did to him.

He had never seen her again. That summer she had left Paris and in the autumn she did not return. Tartaro went to her apartment where a one-eyed American gruffly told him that Miriam was studying privately now and would not return to the Sorbonne. Tartaro asked if the man would forward a letter to her, but when he told the man his name he found the door slammed in his face.

'You're lucky I don't fillet you alive,' the man shouted from inside the apartment.

Later that day he wrote to her with his apologies for his behaviour and posted the letter through her apartment door. If the letter reached her she never replied.

And it was on that afternoon, ironically, that he had first spoken to Grace Matthews. She called herself Grace Rogers in those days and he had seen her around often enough, knew from Miriam that the young girl with the long red hair was an actress of some sort, and a little strange though nice enough. She was standing in the street outside Miriam's apartment block.

'I'm trying to find Miriam,' he said to her.

'But Miriam is not to be found,' the girl said.

Tartaro asked her if she knew how he might contact Charles Monk. The girl hissed and clawed at him like a wild animal, then ran inside the building.

For a while Tartaro overcame his obsession. He threw himself into his studies, took up art history with a special interest in war art and photojournalism. He wrote a thesis on the subject. He did it without thinking, and it came as a shock to him when one of his tutors described Charles Monk as the most interesting of the living war artists, and a subject fit for study.

'I suppose I had forgotten to think of him as such,' Tartaro said to his tutor.

'Because he's still alive or because he doesn't paint tanks? Meet me in the Pompidou tomorrow morning. I'll show you what I mean.'

'This is a recent one,' his tutor said. 'From nineteen-sixty-eight. I recommended the purchase myself.'

It was called *Some Eyes Condemn* – after some English war poet, his tutor said – and was an apparently simple portrait of a man, his jaw slack and his eyes staring listlessly into the distance directly behind the viewer. The one curious effect was that although the man's eyes followed the viewer around the room, there was no sense of being observed by the painting. The condemning eyes might have been sightless.

'It is a shell-shocked American soldier, painted during the siege of Khe Sanh. Monk was there for over a month with the Americans. You'll recall that they were under siege by forty thousand North Vietnamese troops who were themselves under sustained artillery and air barrage. You can't imagine the amount of explosive used. More, I would guess, than in the entire war against Germany. But what do you see?'

Tartaro studied the painting for an hour, managed to transport himself into it – or was transported by the work itself – and, at one critical instant, understood what it was that Monk had portrayed: the eyes of a man who was not blind, but whose mind was so battered that all he could now see were the acres of green farmland of his childhood, all he could smell was the sweet scent of summer corn, all he could hear was the clucking of chickens and the snorting of pigs. It was the portrayal of a man who, despite appearances and known circumstances, had reached a level of profound tranquillity, transcendent happiness, a state of grace.

'It's as if war has stripped away the pains of adulthood and left only the innocent pleasures of childhood,' Tartaro said to his tutor.

'So you see, although Monk is known never to portray the paraphernalia of war, war remains his subject at all times – how war touches the lives of those who experience it. What does this teach us about our lives, about war itself? I had the honour to observe a sitting where Monk drew some rudimentary sketches of Sartre. This would have been during the *événements* and just after Monk was at Khe Sanh. Sartre wanted to hear about the bombardment, so Monk spoke of it as he sketched. At the end Sartre had one comment. He said that on a metaphysical level there was no difference between the experience of being under constant bombardment in a war zone, and the everyday experience of life in the modern Western city. He was just ripping off the Situs, of course. But you know what Monk said? "I'd take a war zone any day. At least there you get some sleep." We all laughed about it, but he was not joking.'

'I met him once,' Tartaro said.

'So I heard,' his tutor said. 'But you can put all that behind you now.'

By the time Tartaro had completed his degree, his obsession with Miriam Janssen had faded to a dim-enough memory and he had met and married a beautiful young Vietnamese refugee. They set up home in the suburbs. Tartaro wrote a well-regarded collection of stories and a monograph on the photography of Robert Capa. He secured a staff position as a critic for a national daily. His life was going as planned. But in nineteen-seventy-four his wife was killed in a Red Army Faction raid on the Paris bank where she worked.

Tartaro was devastated by her death. He resigned his post at the newspaper, sold the house in the suburbs and moved into a one-room apartment in the Pigalle. He spent his days walking the streets or sitting outside cafés, threw himself into his reading, learnt to speak English, German and Italian fluently as a means of escaping himself. He found that he could subsist adequately without a regular job, could live the dissolute life of a student by posing as an impoverished poet and securing the favours of older women in return for companionship, sometimes even physicality, but then only if they had not lost their looks or gone thoroughly to seed.

It was May of the following year that a newspaper article caught his attention. Saigon had finally fallen and there was a photograph of one of the last helicopters to leave before the North Vietnamese overran the American Embassy compound. Charles Monk's grim, misshapen features stared defiantly into the camera lens.

It was a turning point in Tartaro's life, a moment where the machismo he had learnt from his father asserted itself in the place of his mother's romantic sensitivity and he understood that his wife's death was not the end of his life, but the end of one phase of it, that he had been set free to embark on another. If Charles Monk could spend his life in the war zones and disaster areas of the world he, Claude Tartaro, could do so as well. He resolved to work as a freelance correspondent and through his old colleagues at the newspaper secured, after some months, his first commission. He would travel to Indonesia where it was believed that Suharto planned to invade East Timor.

Tartaro never reached East Timor, but spent a month under house arrest in his cheap hotel in the centre of Jakarta. He never learnt who, but someone had tipped off the authorities about his former communist leanings. He returned to Paris dejected. The staff at the newspaper were sympathetic, but they made it clear that he should stick to the arts. The life of an adventurer was not for him, they said, and they hoped he'd got it out of his system. He could have his old job back if that was what he wanted. He took the job and was soon promoted to Arts Editor of the newspaper where he could cover what he wished and take life easy.

With time on his hands, he was at liberty to indulge his rekindled obsession with Charles Monk's life and career. He used the newspaper's facilities to keep track of Monk's movements, carried regular features about him and his paintings and his sometimes obscure, often provocative utterances.

As the years went by Tartaro's collection of cuttings and prints of Monk's works grew until, quite unexpectedly, he found that he had the makings of a book, a new monograph perhaps. He began work on it in earnest, decided that he must see for himself as many of Monk's paintings as possible.

And he never once forgot Miriam Janssen, used the newspaper to follow the fortunes of the Janssen family. By the time Olaf Janssen died, Tartaro felt he knew the family so well that he wept with them; when, in nineteen-eighty, Miriam and Lars Janssen were killed in the explosion which sank their boat the *Ringhorn*, Tartaro was beside himself with grief. He wept for Monk, for the Janssens' children, and most of all for the fact that Monk's painting of Miriam Janssen as she was when he knew her was now beyond him for ever.

In the autumn of nineteen-eighty-five Tartaro was invited to annotate the catalogue for a minor Monk retrospective at the Pompidou – organised without the cooperation of the artist who had been declared, unofficially by the Directorate of Territorial Security, *persona non grata* after expressing his support for Action Directe following the group's bombing the previous year of the European Space Agency.

The exhibition was a success, not least because the outrage caused by Monk's comments meant that Tartaro, *de facto* Paris expert on Monk's paintings, was invited for interview almost on a daily basis by this newspaper or magazine or that television or radio station.

'It's Monk's art I'm interested in. His opinions are of no concern. The artist has no duty to any arbitrary moral codes,' Tartaro repeated himself, again and again.

It was after one such interview that a lilac-scented envelope arrived in his mailbox with an invitation to lunch at a château in the suburbs. 'I have information which may be of interest to you,' the letter said.

Tartaro, curious, sent his acceptance and on the appointed day made his way to Kurt Nowak's elegant home. A butler dressed in a housecoat and wearing a pinafore led him through the house and gardens to a large conservatory gazebo where Nowak, smoking through a long ivory cigarette holder and drinking pink champagne, was occasionally tossing pieces of bread into a large ornamental pond for goldfish lethargically to mumble at.

'They're drunk!' Nowak exclaimed when Tartaro reached him. 'They've had a whole bottle of champagne today and they're drunk! Don't look so shocked, Tartaro, it's a tradition with us. Always get the goldfish drunk! They're no fun otherwise, you know. Nowak. Kurt Nowak.'

He held out a grey-tinged hand for a fleeting fingertip touch before falling back on to his chaise longue and motioning to Tartaro to take a seat.

'I don't have long, you know,' Nowak said.

'Then say what you have to say.'

Tartaro was abrupt and businesslike, fearing that his time had been wasted. Suddenly Nowak tugged his hair and it came away in his hand: a wig. He grinned baldly.

'The chemo, you know.'

'I'm sorry.'

'Champagne? Some cherries, perhaps? They're really very good.'

'Do you have a brother?' Nowak asked him, later. Tartaro was startled by the sudden intensity of the man's tone and gaze.

'A sister,' he said.

'I had a brother. Jean-Louis. He was older than I. He'd lived a life even before I was born. He fought in the Spanish Civil War, in the Eleventh International Brigade, the battalion *Commune de Paris*. After that he flew with a Polish squadron out of England. Our father was a Pole.

And when the war was over and I was born he started making movies. Artistic movies, cutting edge, new wave. He was obsessed with Hollywood, with hardboiled. He had his weaknesses. He had a weakness for young girls – sometimes a little too young. He had a lousy temper, he was obsessive about filmmaking at the expense of everything, even his own life. But he was my big brother. And in nineteen-sixty-four, on the orders of a man who, it has to be said, Jean-Louis owed a little money to, he was murdered – shot down in cold blood by a teenage kid who went by the name of Short Order on account of his height and the fact that he worked as a short-order chef on his godfather's yacht.'

Tartaro's heart began to pound as the implication of these words sank in. Nowak refreshed Tartaro's glass and then his own.

'I see that I have your interest, Tartaro. To the good. To the good.'

'You have proof of this? Why didn't you go to the police?'

'Olaf Janssen had more convincing arguments than a teenage Charles Monk at his disposal. You need to know that.'

Nowak stirred his champagne with a swizzle-stick, sucked the swizzle-stick dry, sipped champagne.

'I want my brother to be remembered, Tartaro, that's all. I want you to write about him in your newspaper – not about his death, not about the people who killed him – but about his life, about what he did, about the films he made, about the talent the world lost twenty-one years ago this summer. If you don't want to write it yourself, just pay someone else to write it. All I ask is that you make sure Jean-Louis isn't forgotten while his killer gets famous for praising terrorists.

'And in return I'll tell you the story of my brother's murder by Charles Monk. It means nothing to me and I can promise you that you'll feel no need to share it with anyone else, not if you value your life. But perhaps for you the trade is fair?'

'There was a real buzz in Europe in those days, you know. So many great filmmakers, so many great films out of Italy, France, Spain, Sweden. Who needed Hollywood? All of us thought we could take on the world, show the Yanks a thing or two. Even show them how to make their own movies. Other people jumped on the bandwagon pretty quickly – Corbucci, Damiani, Leone. They all did the same thing: made Westerns here in Europe. But the idea was my brother's. He thought of it first, he invented the Spaghetti Western. He may not have been the first one to do it, but he had the idea before anyone else. Ask anyone, they'll tell you.

'Jean-Louis wanted more than endless gunfights and blood everywhere and silent strangers riding into town, though. His idea was to make a whole commentary on the Western, build a set that was practically a real town, actually colonise some hostile place in just the way the early frontier settlers did when they headed west. And he didn't want to hide from people that this was a movie, that it was fiction. So some of the set would be real and it would be filmed as it was. Other bits would not be real but they would be filmed as if they were. And then throughout there would be glimpses of the unreality of it all. You would discover that the town's largest hotel was simply a façade with nothing beyond it but desert. Or the fact that the bank had four façades, only one of them the façade of a bank, the other three of I don't know what – whorehouse, general store, barbershop, whatever. Do you know just how resistant the Western form is to irony?

'We had a plot. A simple plot. You know the story of Polyphemus and Acis and Gala? OK. Polyphemus you know, the one-eyed giant who ruled Sicily and was blinded by Ulysses. But before that he was in love with a beautiful nymph called Galatea. And Galatea was in love with a beautiful satyr called Acis. So Polyphemus crushed Acis to death with a rock and Acis was turned into a river. And Galatea threw herself into the ocean to be with her lover for ever.

'It was a great basis for a movie. A Bad Man loves a Good Woman, a Good Woman loves a Good Man who loves her, the Bad Man kills the Good Man, the Good Woman kills herself. You couldn't ask for more. It has love, it has death, it has resonance, it has dynamics. There was even a score for it. Handel. Morricone's heart could bleed dry for all we cared.

'I was to play Ace, a cardsharp who's fallen in love with a young girl, a prostitute called Gala. The two of them have found redemption through love, they're ready to turn their backs on the bad ways they've gone. They want to head out to Oregon, grab some land and live happily ever after with kids and a milk cow called Daisy and a porch for sitting in the evenings.

'Things don't work out that way. There's a one-eyed outlaw, a Mexican bandit called El Ojo who's been terrorising the region for years. El Ojo and his men ride into town. They've heard that a gold shipment is heading that way and El Ojo wants to hijack it. Ace and Gala lay low, they try to stay out of trouble, but one night El Ojo pitches up at the saloon. He wants to play poker. Ace can't resist it. He sees his chance to shoot the moon, take this outlaw for every penny he and Gala need for their new life.

'And meanwhile El Ojo's eye is caught by Gala. He pursues her and when she resists his advances, tells him she's in love with the man who just cleaned him out at the poker table, El Ojo arranges to meet Ace in a canyon outside town. There's a huge thunderstorm. El Ojo blows the canyon walls with dynamite, Ace is killed. When Gala hears the news she rides out to the canyon which by now has been turned into a raging torrent by a flash flood. She throws herself into it.

'We had a script, even a location high up in the Sierra Nevada. What we did not have was the money to make the film, or a lead actress to star in it. The money, that was never going to be a problem. The lead actress, though, she took us five years to find.

'We were at the station in Milan when Jean-Louis saw her. We were late for the train back to Paris and he had to get back for a meeting, so he pointed her out to me, told me to do whatever it took to get her to come to Paris for a screen test. She was a tough-looking kid, maybe ten, eleven years old, long red hair, no make-up, no jewellery, silver sandals – I remember those. They killed me. I just showed her a hundred bucks and that was it. We overnighted in Monte Carlo. I bought her some clothes. She could have passed for someone twice her age. I took her to a casino. The next day we were in Paris. I left her at the hotel for a few hours and told her to get anything she wanted on my account. By the time I got back she had bought a goldfish and a bowl to keep it in. She was wired up the wrong way, but cute with it. She killed me.

'The next day I brought her out here in time for breakfast. I fed her smoked salmon and champagne. Jean-Louis brought the coffee in himself. "The Scots know a thing or two about breakfast and fish," he said. "But for coffee, only the Italians make coffee worth drinking." He knew how to lay it on. By the end of the morning he had her eating out of his hand. Strawberries. She'd never had them before, she said. She wasn't Italian at all, but British. We never did find out her real name or how she ended up alone in Milan, but she called herself Grace. She was some kid.

'The screen test worked out. She was perfect for the part. So Jean-Louis got to work on the money. You know how it is, Tartaro. You can always get some money from somewhere, even big money, even when it's crazy money for a crazy idea – you can always get it one way or another. As I said, Jean-Louis fought in Spain, stayed there a month too long, until the only way out was to go by sea. It happened that the man who agreed to take him was Olaf Janssen.

'They got on with each other, went on a week-long bender in Marseille when they landed there. Janssen let it slip that he was connected – a bit more than just connected. He told my brother that if he ever needed anything, if he ever had any problem, he should just go to Janssen and whatever he needed would be provided; whatever problem he had would be made to go away. In return, as a favour in advance, my brother gave Janssen a list of the names and addresses of every person he had met in the International Brigades – people who would always offer help to any friend of his. A man called George Monk who was a machine-gunner in the *Edgar André* in Madrid was on that list. A year later Janssen was in London. He shot a cop. It was George Monk who helped him out of the scrape, saved his neck. All because Janssen said he was a friend of Jean-Louis Nowak.

'It was nearly thirty years before my brother needed to call in his favour. Janssen was the big shot by then. No one could get near him, no one could reach him except through the official channel – George Monk. Jean-Louis called Monk up, eventually reached him, Monk talked to Janssen, Janssen yessed it. This should have been a good thing. It wasn't. When the money was wired to the company account, there was only one tenth of what Janssen had agreed to invest. Then we got a call from a man named William Rogers. He would deliver the rest of the money in person. In cash. Of course we understood right away what that meant. Janssen didn't want to make an investment. He wanted to offload dirty money and leave it to us to wash it clean. It happens all the time.

'Rogers turned up the next day with a couple of million in cash. Incidentally, he said, he'd always liked the idea of acting in a movie. Besides which, Janssen wanted an eye kept on his investment – an eye being literal because Rogers only had one eye. My brother, dumb fuck that he sometimes could be, cast Rogers as El Ojo on the spot. And it's true that he looked the part.'

*

'Grace and Jean-Louis and I rode up to the set on horseback. It was a three-day journey. Jean-Louis wanted us to see it for the first time through the eyes of our characters. He wanted us to be our characters for the whole time that we were there. She would call me Ace, I would call her Gala, and Jean-Louis was the Undertaker if he was called anything at all. He'd cast himself as the town's undertaker. All very symbolic, you understand.

'Jean-Louis had built a whole town from nothing. There was a wide boulevard lined with tall wooden buildings, narrow sidestreets making a ragged edge to the east and west and north. And to the south a gradual meta-morphosis, from western frontier town, to Mexican pueblo. Whitewashed walls, a big church, goats and chickens in the streets. And beyond the town, on a low hill, there was the graveyard surrounded by a white picket fence. They called the place Fuego. Fire.

'Nothing there was as it seemed. The bank was actually the canteen for cast and crew. The livery stables were just a huge storehouse filled with tumbleweed made from painted, tangled fusewire. And beyond the doors of the hardware store there was only the mesa itself, the high sierras in the distance.

'There were problems with Rogers from the start. Any idiot could tell that Jean-Louis's spending was out of control. Everything had to be flown up there, even the water was flown up, and food, twice a day. Rogers told him: you fuck this up, you're a dead man. I was there. I heard him say it.

'We had kept Grace away from Rogers until we got there. At first it was fine. He thought she was too young to act the lead, but he looked out for her, spent time with her when Jean-Louis was busy with one thing or another. But then he found out that Jean-Louis was screwing her. It was downhill from there. You can't make a film when one of your main actors is accidentally punching you in the kidneys every time he walks past.

'There were other things too. One of the key scenes in the movie came after Ace has cleaned out El Ojo, and El Ojo and his men rampage through the town, rob the bank, burn down a church. The fire spread, and instead of cutting, Jean-Louis made everyone keep filming. Half the town got burnt, the crew quarters included. It looked great when it was printed, but it pissed people off.

'And there was a bigger problem. Jean-Louis had been told, I don't know who by, but he had been promised that every April the rains came to the mesa and flooded the canyon where the final scenes were to be filmed – firstly Grace throwing herself into the river, then the Hollywood ending, the good guys stampeding a thousand head of cattle through El Ojo's camp, all of them and El Ojo's men plunging into the ravine and drowning.

'By April nearly everything was in the can and the rushes were looking great. The cattle had arrived and we just needed the rain. But the money was gone, no more food or water was being flown up, no more fuel, nothing. And the rain didn't come. Jean-Louis kept telling everyone that it would come – any day now, he kept saying. But they had nothing to eat or drink, we were running low on cigarettes, booze, it was cold up there, they could see they'd never get paid. The crew started to leave first, packed what they could on to the horses and left. Then the cast started to go. Rogers said he would be back. Finally there was just me, Grace and Jean-Louis. The rain never came.'

Nowak paused to light a cigarette and refill their glasses. For a long moment he studied Tartaro suspiciously.

'You promise me you'll write this article?'

'Or commission someone else to do so, yes. You have my word.'

'Very well.'

Throughout that summer the sun shone with brutal intensity and the wind blew with a cold, relentless violence. The town began to dilapidate. The fire-damaged buildings crumbled to ash and the days were filled with the sounds of falling masonry. One day the livery stables crashed to the ground and the fake tumbleweed which had been stored there blew across the mesa like baby spiders on the wind.

The three of them moved into the Mexican district. The walls were thicker, the interiors cooler, though there too the buildings creaked and groaned, foundationless on the shifting sands of the mesa.

In the American district only the saloon was safe. HQ, built to last. Nowak spent his days there alone, waiting. Kurt would ride out in the morning with a shotgun or rifle or both and return towards dusk with a rabbit or a goat or a wild pig. Grace tended the graves in the cemetery, started a garden there, kept the white picket fence in good repair and freshly painted. She learnt to bake bread in a clay oven and cook bean and rabbit stew over an open fire. There was no fuel for the generator. The water from the well tasted of copper and tar. Every morning she would walk with Nowak into the American district and he would help her gather the dry and brittle wood which had splintered from the buildings.

At night they would gather by the fire for warmth and pass a bottle of whiskey round. They spoke little, but now and again Nowak or Kurt would reminisce or construct a scene or a plot for a movie.

In the autumn Nowak started spending longer in the American district, not returning at night or for days on end. One day Grace was fetching water from the well when the sound of hammering started up near by. She found him in one of the workshops banging nails into planks.

'I'm making coffins,' he said. 'Just in case.'

'Just in case?'

'Just in case.'

'Can't we just leave here?'

'Nowhere to run, nowhere to hide. Besides, we got a movie to wrap.'

Throughout the autumn Nowak worked, building coffin after coffin and stacking them in the town square. When he had used all the scrap wood he could find, he began tearing down the buildings which still stood. Grace took to stealing coffins in the dead of night to use for firewood. One night he caught her. He held a shotgun to her head.

'I might have known you'd be the thief. White trash, that's all you ever were, that's all you'll ever be.'

'We need it for the fire.'

'Just this once I'll let it slide. But from now on you get your own wood.'

The pile of coffins grew. Grace and Kurt spent a week dismantling the remains of the hotel and carting it back to add to the woodpile. One day Kurt noticed that the woodpile was smaller than it should have been. They stood guard and when Nowak came that night Grace held a shotgun to his head.

'Just this once,' she said, 'I'll let it slide. But from now on you get your own wood.'

It became a race with unspoken rules: no power tools, no brute force. Every nail in every plank had to be hammered out and collected in a pile of iron for coffin-making, the planks kept intact. For a week they hardly ate. Finally only the saloon remained standing.

'Not that,' said Kurt.

'No,' said Nowak. 'Not that.'

His gaze drifted to the white picket fence around the graveyard.

'Don't even think about it,' said Grace.

They called a truce and Nowak went back to making coffins, Kurt returned to hunting, Grace tended the graves, cooked and baked. She neglected her garden. There was not enough water and nothing would grow.

In the winter the snow came. Kurt stopped hunting and inventoried everything they had. Enough, but barely, to last until spring. Nowak made coffins and stacked them ever higher in the town square, but he started eating with them again, and sleeping in their house. He wanted to sleep with Grace.

'Fuck you,' she said. 'If you think I'm a cow you can visit once a year you can think again.'

'I'm not cut out to be a monk,' said Nowak. 'Don't do this to me.'

'There's a goat in the stable,' she said. 'Go fuck that.'

Nowak killed the goat and they roasted it whole on Christmas Day.

In the spring the snow and ice melted and the ground softened. Grace was tending the graves one day when Nowak arrived, pickaxe in one hand, a shovel in the other. She squared up to him.

'I'm going to dig some graves,' he said.

'New ones, I hope.'

'New ones. Just in case.'

Kurt started hunting again. They ate fresh meat every day but they ran out of coffee. Grace tended the graves and repaired the white picket fence, gave it a fresh coat of paint. She baked bread and she cooked. Nowak dug holes in the earth, six feet deep.

One day Kurt came back early from hunting and rode straight to the saloon to find Nowak. Grace was sitting with him, drinking tea. Kurt and his brother spoke privately for a moment, then they dragged her biting and kicking and screaming to a windowless storeroom near her home and locked her in. She would never see Jean-Louis Nowak again.

'We knew they wanted him, not me or Grace. It was just a question of settling terms – what would happen to us. Of course Jean-Louis tried to talk Janssen out of it, tried to tell him the movie could still get wrapped, but Janssen wasn't listening. He'd brought his boy up with him, and Charles Monk. No sign of Rogers, but we guessed he'd be somewhere near by. The boys had to be blooded, that was what it was all about.

'Jean-Louis tried to talk Janssen out of it, then he talked to Monk. He spent hours talking to Monk. Monk didn't listen. In the end Jean-Louis gave up. I covered him with a shotgun while he bashed Monk about a bit, nothing too serious, just to remind him that he was still a kid and that Jean-Louis was the man.

'We walked a while, then he told me to go check on Grace. By the time I found him again his brains had been blown out and they'd left him to rot.'

Nowak slumped back on the chaise longue and waved his hand at the now-empty champagne bottle. The butler appeared moments later with a fresh one, opened it and filled their glasses.

'But you don't know,' Tartaro said.

Nowak stared at him blankly.

'You have no proof that it was Monk who killed your brother. You didn't see him do it.'

'It was him. Janssen had no need to get his hands dirty and his boy didn't have the balls, you could see that at a glance. It was Monk who murdered my brother, Tartaro. There's no question in my mind about that.'

'Dig up what you can, Claude,' his editor said to him, 'but forget about holding your breath. The Janssens are dead and Monk's hardly going to tell you anything. This Nowak character could be anyone. Have you checked his side of it out?'

A sound engineer told Tartaro of fiery arguments between Jean-Louis Nowak and Buck Rogers – a Janssen stooge, the man said.

'There was no doubt in my mind that Rogers would have killed Nowak in an instant if he thought he could get away with it. Of course we all knew Nowak was screwing the lead, and of course she was too young. But you see that all the time, it's nothing new. Rogers overreacted. That's all.'

From one of the actors, **Tartaro** obtained a script of the film. It was garbage, even his untrained eye could see that.

'You're missing the point,' the actor said to him. 'Of course it was garbage. It was all a big scam to rip off Janssen. Don't ask me where the percentage in it was because I don't know. But I'll bet that's what it was all about.'

Another member of the cast was less certain.

'To tell the truth I think he had lost it. He made one decent film and that was all he had in him. That's the problem with these *auteur* filmmakers. Am-*auteur* if you want my opinion.'

Had any of the cast or crew encountered Charlie Monk, he wanted to know. All he got was blank faces.

'I know who he is but Rogers was Janssen's only man on the spot and I'd bet money that it was him who did the old SOB in. He had the look of a killer, that one.'

Convinced nevertheless that he had the makings of a big story, Tartaro asked his editor for permission to fly to Spain to investigate further. Memories of his only previous foreign assignment had not faded.

'I'm sorry, Claude. But I'll tell you what I'll do. We have a correspondent in Seville. He'll be in Paris next week. You can tell him what it is you need to know and we'll see what he turns up. If there's a story in it, it's yours, but I'm not having another report on one month in a crappy hotel room.'

Disappointed but not surprised, Tartaro briefed the Spaniard. For a month he heard nothing, then his editor called him into his office.

'It's as well I didn't let you go down there. Luiz is banged up on some bullshit spying charge and last night I got rousted by half-a-dozen bastards from External Security telling me to lay off anything to do with the Janssens. I said to the bastards it was Monk we were looking at, and they said, same thing. Monk is Janssen. So it looks like you're on to something. I shouldn't let it go, but they've got my balls in a vice. I'm sorry, Claude.'

When the Spanish correspondent was finally released he faxed a single page to Tartaro. The gist of it was simple.

Spanish Air Force records showed that a light aircraft was sent into the mountains south of Granada on the twenty-third of July, nineteen-sixty-four and that it flew with a single passenger straight to a military hospital near Ronda where a young adult male was treated for severe facial injuries. No further information was available.

'It's corroboration of sweet fuck-all, Claude,' his editor said to him. 'We can't accuse a man of murder just because we can prove someone duffed him up a bit. Look, perhaps you can prove that Monk was up there. That's something. But you need more. You need to work around the story. Get what you can. To start with, find the girl. And do it on your own time, Claude. This is old piss, and those bastards are still watching me.'

Nowak's actress had disappeared, it seemed, from the face of the earth. Tartaro discovered quickly that she had been adopted by Buck Rogers, whom he assumed to be the one-eyed American he had encountered twenty years earlier in Miriam Janssen's Paris apartment. Grace Rogers had lived in the same apartment block until nineteen-seventy when the lease reverted to Janssen Shipping. She no longer appeared in the council records as living in Paris, or at least not under the name Rogers. With his own money Tartaro hired a detective agency to find the girl. They found no trace of her.

Tartaro was not dismayed. It seemed to him that he had been seeking some truth about Miriam Janssen and Charles Monk for two decades and that his investigation was destined to follow its own course, that its progress was something over which he had only minimal control. The truth would be revealed in the fullness of time. He had only to remain patient and to continue with his work.

His monograph on the works of Charles Monk had become the makings of a full-length biography; publishers had got wind of it and every month he received approaches from one editor or another keen to see the manuscript.

'I haven't completed my research,' he said.

'You could release it in two volumes,' they would say.

'Publish now what you have and later what you still need to discover.'

'No,' he would say. 'The research I am undertaking relates to Monk's early life. It would not be appropriate. You'll just have to wait.'

It gave him pleasure to be courted by these people, though he knew well enough that the glory was reflected. It was the facts of Charles Monk's life with which these editors were obsessed. Tartaro felt no resentment. The glory, when the truth was revealed, would be his and his alone.

In nineteen-eighty-nine there was an incident. He had been visited by an editor from a British publisher, an absurd donkey of a figure with shoulder-length hair who talked of million-pound deals and praised Tartaro's monograph on Robert Capa in terms which left it quite clear that the man had never read the book, perhaps any book, in his life. Tartaro had excused himself midway through their lunch and left the restaurant without so much as a backwards glance.

When he got back to his apartment he fed his dog as usual, then prepared to take the animal for its lunchtime walk, a long-standing routine whereby they would stroll through the park close to his home and then Tartaro would drink a coffee at his favourite café on the corner of the park before returning by a slightly different route which took them past the bookshop where he would often browse for a few minutes, leaving the dog tied up outside.

He had the sense throughout the walk that day that the dog was nervous, that someone was watching them both.

He shook it off, drank his coffee, visited the bookshop. When he came out, the dog was gone. It was not the first time it had happened and the dog had always found its way home in the past, so he went directly to his apartment to change before going to work for the afternoon.

The creature was laid out on the bed, spreadeagled on its back, its underside slashed from its throat to its pelvis, entrails bubbling from its stomach, a bloodstain spreading across the cream-coloured bedspread. Attached to the collar there was a note:

HUNGER AS A MOTIVATING FACTOR IN THE ISSUE OF WAR, PART II

1989. Flesh and blood on cotton. 150 × 210 cm. Dead dog spreadeagled on cotton bedspread with stomach slashed open. Private collection of M. Claude Tartaro: Gift of the artist.

NOTES: The symbolism of the mutilated corpse of his own dog being left on his own bed was not lost on the critic for whom this unusual work was specially created. A clear message from artist to critic, the work serves as an invitation to the critic to consider his own mortality in the context of his current investigations.

Tartaro could not imagine that Monk himself had done this; he suspected the hand of the Security services or simply a Janssen Shipping hired-thug. He took photographs of the scene but did not report it to the police.

The incident chilled him, yet thrilled him beyond

words. If his investigation had attracted the attention of Monk himself, or of Monk's associates, then surely this vindicated his search, indicated that Monk's dark past was within his grasp. But he was made cautious. In an interview with an American art magazine he implied that he had given up on Charles Monk as a subject for his writing.

'Monk is a brilliant artist, among the most brilliant of our times, and a fascinating and complex figure, but for any writer there are times when it is better to focus on one's own creative work.'

As chance had it, Tartaro had been working on a novel and it was all but complete. He sold it to a publisher for a reasonable sum and announced that he would now concentrate on writing fiction. He left his job at the newspaper and, true to his word, embarked on a second novel and wrote occasional pieces for magazines, but otherwise lived the obsure life of a middle-aged man of French letters.

He quietly continued his research and one year after receiving that warning message even dared to attend the unveiling of a new work by Monk at the Pompidou. 4.669 was a stunning portrait of one of the students involved in the previous year's protests in Tiananmen Square. The subject of the portrait had the image of a butterfly tattooed or painted on to his face in lavish detail, and the work was a riot of colours and textures which celebrated the successful aspects of the protests as much as it highlighted human frailty in the face of totalitarian power. Monk was at the unveiling but did not speak, just sat by the painting in silence, surveying the room from behind dark sun-glasses. Tartaro avoided his eye.

He had not come to the ceremony in search of any specific clues as to the whereabouts of Grace Rogers, but after the speeches he fell into conversation with a man he remembered meeting in his student days, a poet called Alain Morand who had fallen on hard times in recent years.

They discussed the painting and agreed that it was a masterpiece, commented sardonically on the assembled Philistines and, as people began to leave, agreed to drink a glass of wine together in a nearby café.

'I would like to say that it's poet's block,' Morand explained. 'But it seems to be more than that. I haven't been able to write a line since nineteen-eighty.'

'What sparked it off?' Tartaro asked.

'Two things. In the first place I read Lautréamont. No, really, I'd never read him before and to come across him at that age was surprisingly damaging to me. You remember the scandal when I was accused of plagiarising and in my defence I stated that it was less plagiarism than alteration, updating. You'll recall my arguments were accepted. No one told me that even that idea had been conceived before.'

'It must be possible to go beyond Lautréamont, surely. His writing is for adolescents.'

'Of course, but that's the point. If I'd read him when I was younger it would be done with, forgotten. But there was another matter. You must remember Miriam Janssen. Of course you do. You were the only one of us with the gumption to try your hand with her.'

'It ended badly.'

'And she came to a bad end. Her death still haunts me. It's bad enough when anyone who's touched your life dies, but when a beautiful woman whose face you've studied a thousand times dies in such a brutal way, well, between that and Ducasse, my soul was under attack. I haven't written a line since.'

'I wonder, do you remember an acquaintance of Miriam's, a young girl called Grace? I used to see her around now and again. I'd like to trace her.'

'Of course.' Morand tapped his forehead twice. 'Completely insane. I could never see why Miriam took her under her wing as she did.'

'How do you mean?'

'As I heard it, the girl wanted to escape her adopted father. It wasn't that there was bad blood between them, just that she felt oppressed by the attentions of any man. Miriam set her up with a place in Granada. I heard she spent nearly every day in the Generalife – which I can understand. It's got healing qualities, that place.'

'And now? Do you know where she is now?'

'I haven't got a clue. There was some suggestion she was on the boat when it sank. You know they never salvaged it, so we'll never know.'

'I always wondered about that. I'd have thought they would have wanted to give them all a proper burial.'

'The waters off Cartagena are pretty deep.'

Tartaro went home dispirited. If Grace Rogers were truly dead, the mystery of Jean-Louis Nowak's death might never be solved. But as he lay awake that night it seemed to him that she could not be dead, that his destiny was too bound up with finding her for her to be dead and he alive. Once again he decided that patience was his best ally, that the truth would come to him and that seeking it out at this stage would bring no benefit.

FIVE

GOATFUCK

1991. Oil on canvas, 46.6 × 35.4 cm. Portrait of dead Iraqi conscript with half of head missing. Private collection.

NOTES: Title, American service slang for a large-scale foul-up, caused widespread offence among Muslims in Britain and abroad – to which Monk's infamous retort was 'Let them fuck goats.' Work is unusual in its portrayal of violent death and is among the most didactic of Monk's *oeuvre*. His opposition to the American action against Iraq was eclipsed only by his horror at the sterility of the media coverage of war, and he felt a resulting need to portray the realism of death on the battlefield in as graphic a manner as possible.

Claude Tartaro, Page 172.

Béatrice had fallen asleep again. Monk made himself coffee and took it out on to the balcony where he sat looking down on to Russia Street.

'*Les pertubations, les anxiétés, les dépravations, la mort, les exceptions dans l'ordre physique ou moral, l'esprit de négation, les abrutissements, les hallucinations servies par la volonté, les tourments, la destruction, les renversements, les larmes, les insatiabilités, les asservissements, les imaginations creusantes, les romans, ce qui est inattendu, ce qu'il ne faut pas faire, les singularités chimiques de vautour mystérieux qui guette la charogne de quelque illusion morte, les expériences précoces et avortées, les obscurités à carapace de punaise, la monomanie terrible de l'orgueil, l'inoculation des stupeurs profundes, les oraisons funèbres, les envies, les trahisons, les tyrannies, les impiétés, les irritations, les acrimonies, les incartades agressives, la démence, le spleen, les épouvantements raisonnés, les inquiétudes étranges, que le lecteur préférerait ne pas éprouver, les grimaces, les névroses, les filières sanglantes par lesquelles on fait passer la logique aux abois, les exagérations, l'absence de sincérité, les scies, les platitudes, le sombre, le lugubre, les enfantements pires que les meurtres, les passions, le clan des romanciers de cours d'assises, les tragédies, les odes, les mélodrames, les extrêmes présentés à perpétuité, la raison impunément sifflée, les odeurs de poule mouillée, les affadissements, les grenouilles, les poulpes, les requins, le simoun des déserts, ce qui est somnambule, louche, nocturne, somnifère, noctambule, visqueux, phoque parlant, équivoque, poitrinaire, spasmodique, aphrodisiaque, anémique, borgne, hermaphrodite, bâtard, albinos, pédéraste, phénomène d'aquarium et femme à barbe, les heures soûles du découragement taciturne, les fantaisies, les âcretés, les monstres, les syllogismes démoralisateurs, les ordures, ce qui ne réfléchit pas comme l'enfant, la désolation, ce mancenillier intellectuel, les chancres parfumés, les cuisses aux camélias, la culpabilité d'un écrivain qui roule sur la pente du néant et se méprise lui-même avec des cris joyeux, les remords, les hypocrisies, les perspectives vagues qui vous broient dans leurs engrenages imperceptibiles, les crachats sérieux sur les axiomes sacrés, la vermine et ses chatouillements insinuants, les préfaces insensées, comme celles de Cromwell, de Mlle de Maupin et de Dumas fils, les caducités, les impuissances, les blasphèmes, les asphyxies, les étouffements, les rages, – devant ces charniers immondes, que je rougis de nommer, il est temps de réagir enfin contre ce qui nous choque et nous courbe si souverainement,'* he said to the street.

The street sighed, had heard it all before.

The road into the mountains had begun as a sweeping brushstroke across the landscape of the foothills; by the time they reached the mesa it was a scrabbling, hypoxic track. The horses were tired and sweating despite the cold, their heads beginning to drop.

At the foot of a low rise on the mesa's edge there was a

signboard propped against a wooden post. The lettering on it was etched as a negative where the paint had long since flaked from the sunbleached wood:

FUEGO-FIRE

'Keep on truckin' boys,' Olaf murmured.

The three of them – he, Lars and Olaf – rode into what had once been a town, their handguns at the ready.

They found Nowak sitting on top of a pile of coffins in the centre of the town square. Nowak was dressed in a tailcoat with dress-trousers and brogues. He had a battered top hat on his head and a tailor's tape-measure dangling from around his neck. He stared at them for a long time as they took in the desolation.

'There are real graves in the graveyard,' Nowak said.

Monk and Lars, sensing a threat, fingered their triggers and looked around warily.

'You can tell which the real ones are because the grass grows greener on them, and in the spring mountain flowers take root.'

Olaf dismounted and handed the reins of his horse to Lars.

'Where your brother, Nowak?' he asked.

'He took Grace someplace safe. You ain't gonna hurt them.'

'Not if he make no shit.'

'I thought you might have brought Rogers. He still owes me a scene or two.'

'He on other business for me. Believe it, he like to be here for this.'

'Buy you a drink, Olaf? Got some of that Swedish giggle juice you like. Kept it back, as a matter of fact.'

'Boys, you see to the horses. Me 'n' the Polack are gonna go get drunk.'

By midnight Olaf and Lars had fallen asleep.

'Like father like son, huh? He never could hold his booze. Did he give you the skinny on all this?'

Monk lit a cigarette.

'He just said you owe him money,' he said.

'It's true. I owe him a shitload of money. It cost a shitload to build this place, of course it did. We had to fly everything up here, all the materials, the workers, the supplies, everything. It cost a goddam shitload. Not much to show for it, either.

'That ain't why I gotta be waxed. He'd get his jack back. If jack was all it was he'd get his jack back in the end. Goddamn flick was just about wrapped. I just needed a few more scenes and it would have been in the can. Hell, if I had the scratch to get my lenser up here for a few more days I probably could still wrap the flick. I just need some rain.'

Nowak took Monk's cigarette from his mouth and crushed it out on the bar top. He handed him a large cigar.

'Ever smoked one of these? Try it. You'll never buy another deck of those Luckies in your life.'

Nowak shook his head and emptied the dregs of the whisky bottle into his glass, tossed the drink back and moved behind the bar to fetch a new bottle.

'It ain't the rhino. You know Buck Rogers? Of course you do. Me 'n' him, we didn't exactly see eye to eye, if you'll forgive. I should never've agreed to let him be in the movie. I always knew it was a mistake. I'm the movie-maker, not Olaf, not Buck Rogers, not anyone. Buck Rogers tried to tell me how I should make my movie. We were always gonna fall out. It ain't the rhino. It's a simple matter of who's got Olaf Janssen's ear, and it sure ain't me. Hell, why am I telling you this? Olaf's got your ear and you sure ain't gonna listen to some washed-up helmer like me no matter how way me and Olaf go back. I'm not a good man, Charlie, and I never said I was. But I can make a film when I have to. That was all I ever wanted to do.

'I know what you're thinking, Charlie. You're thinking why the hell am I just gonna roll over for this. Why ain't I holed up with a rod and squirting metal your way any chance I get? I'll tell you, Charlie, it crossed my mind. The truth of it is, even if I could bop all three of you, Buck Rogers would just send up more goons, a chopper squad, whatever. It'd all get messy. There'd be no point to it. This way I go quiet, painless, and Olaf sees me right, squares things for Grace and Kurt. They don't get pooped, just hoof it back to the pad in Gaul and get on with their lives. That counts for something.

'So, Charlie, who's the trigger man on this one? You? Lars? It surely ain't Olaf. You two're here to earn your buttons, am I right? I thought as much. Just don't make a mess of my mug, that's all I ask. Charlie, you wanna take some air with me? It's a beautiful night and I don't plan on sleeping through it. I'll show you around my town, what's left of it. We can take the hooch with us. Here, I'll freshen your drink before we go.'

*

As dawn gathered they sat on a bench in the cemetery smoking cigars, drinking whisky and staring down over the town.

'So what do you want from your life, Charlie? You wanna make a shitload of sugar? No, sugar you got. Sugar you can always get. Even Olaf never did it for the sugar, even if he did end up with a shnozzle full of the stuff. Sugar ain't where it's at. So what then? Respect? Well, no one likes to be taken for a rube. Of course you need some respect in this life. But you know what the paradox is? If you've got to go out of your way to get it, you can be sure you don't deserve it. You can be sure that some asshole is out there laughing at you and there ain't a damn thing you can do about it. Oh, you can wax them, sure, but it's like a monster: you wax someone who don't show you respect, you get ten other guys laughing at you is the consequence. So what's the point? Respect you either get or you don't, and the less you sweat it the more you get it.

'So what else? The love of a good dame. Of course. Maybe it's someone you carry a torch for for a while, she gives you those gew-gew eyes, that sly come-hither stare. Before you know it you've got her under your skin, she's all you could desire, she'd be so nice to come home to. So you woo her, that ain't so tough: baste a chick well she'll cook easy, am I right? Of course I'm right. You buy her flowers, champagne, take her to dinner, nice and easy does it. And what? She makes you feel young, you're in heaven, your heart beats so you can hardly speak, you're on the road to romance, you're just like a couple of tots – sing along with me, Charlie. And that's the tender trap, that's what it is. I say tomato, you say tomato, but that's what it is: it's the tender trap. You're dizzy with this dame and before you know it you're putting a ring on her finger, she needs more shoes, there's a bambino puking all over your best rags, she got a pussy like I don't wanna even think about. Here, have another cigar if this is unsettling your stomach. You catch my drift, I'm sure. It ain't a pretty picture.

'OK. What else do we got? Fame. Now fame is something special, ain't it? You get the sugar, you get the high-class skirt, you get the respect, you get all that by the shitload. What could be more dandy than fame? I'll tell you, Charlie, I know a famous person or two. I've been to Hollywood, I've hung out with the high-rollers in Vegas, I did all that. And every goddamn one of them is a boozehound or a pussyhound or a hophead or a snowbird or hittin' the pipe or ten-and-a-half other kinds of screw-up – and why? Because the fame, is why. It fucks you right up; you can't live with it. You get famous, you always always always think you're more important than you really are, and because your insignificance hits you at every turn you have to find something – anything – to stave off that sense of your own inadequacy, whether it's the booze or the dope or the endless twist or whatever. Fame fucks you right up, Charlie, and don't you ever forget it.

'We're not getting left with a whole lot here. I'll put you out of your misery: you wanna make art, am I right? Of course I'm right. I can see it in you, the way you look at things, people. You're like me, you see everything in rectangles. That's OK, but that's just the start of it. You gotta ask yourself what the point of it is. Why do you wanna make art if it ain't for the sugar, the respect, the skirt, the fame? It's gotta be for the sake of the art itself, but what's the point of the art? What's it for? What job does it do in this crazy fucked-up world we live in? You think about that, Charlie.

'And you know, Charlie, it ain't easy. The myths, they're all broken now, they don't work right. You wanna make great art in this day and age, you gotta take those broken myths and put them right back together again. You can't put them back the way they were before, but you gotta put them back together the best you can, make them new myths, make them whole. And that's what I was gonna do. That's all I ever wanted to do.'

Nowak shrugged, tapped ash on to the ground, sipped on his whisky.

'It would have been a great little flick, Charlie, a little long in the works it's true, but the auds would have slurped it up. It would have been a groundbreaking movie. The perfs were darb, the lenswork was outta this world; it would have had everything – humanity, tragedy, betrayal, love, everything. But the rain never came. I guess it just wasn't to be.'

Nowak stood and motioned to Monk to stand as well.

'Kurt. You can come out now.'

Kurt Nowak came out from behind a headstone, a revolver in his hand aimed at Monk.

'Now Charlie, grab a little air, not all the way up away from your sides, away from your body, turn around. Don't sweat it, he ain't gonna be pumpin' no lead, not so long as you do what I tell you.'

Nowak undid Monk's trouser belt, pulled it free, then

undid Monk's trousers, let them drop to his ankles. He pulled Monk's arms behind him and roughly tied them with the belt.

'Turn around. I ain't no pug so this won't kill you, just might smart a bit. Bite your teeth together and keep 'em that way if you can. At least don't stick your tongue out.'

Suddenly Nowak stepped forward and punched Monk full on the chin. Monk spat out a tooth and blood.

'Stand up. You OK? Good.'

Nowak punched him again. There was a crunch as Monk's nose broke.

'Stand up. I ain't no pug, but I could kill you easy enough with my bare hands. Bust a kidney, or a hard one right on the ticker, that'd see you off. Don't sweat it, Charlie, that ain't what this is about.'

He punched him again, cutting his eyebrow. Blood flowed but quickly stopped as Monk's eye closed up.

'Stand up.'

He punched him again: his other eye.

'Stand up.'

The nose again, then the chin, one-two.

'Stand up.'

Monk's left cheek: the bone cracked.

'Stand up.'

Monk's right cheek: the bone cracked.

'Stand up. Stand up, you pussy.'

He roundhoused Monk's jaw: it broke.

'Stand up.'

'Jean-Louis!'

Nowak turned and looked at his brother, took a deep

breath and stood back from Monk's body curled up on the ground, nodded.

'Let's walk a while, Kurt. Let's say goodbye.'

Lars found him where they had left him. He helped him to his feet, supported his weight as they walked slowly back to the saloon. He bathed his wounds and bandaged his jaw.

'Where is he?' Monk asked through broken teeth.

'With Olaf. They went riding together; there was something Nowak wanted to show him.'

'He's mine, Lars.'

'I know,' said Lars. 'I think, perhaps, that was the point. I'm going to call Buck on the radio and get him to fly the Cessna up here. We need to get you to hospital.'

When he felt steadier on his feet Monk said he was going for a walk.

'I need some time on my own,' he said.

He found himself in the Mexican district. There was the sound of someone rapping listlessly on the door of one of the buildings. Monk opened the door. She leapt back, holding a stick in front of her.

'It's OK,' he said. 'You have nothing to fear from me.'

She said nothing, cowered when he moved towards her. He stepped back. Then the light from the doorway was obscured. Monk turned. It was Kurt. He was unarmed. Monk drew his revolver and pointed it at him.

'Please leave,' said Kurt. 'She has nothing to do with this.'

Monk waved Kurt aside and walked out of the building and back to the saloon.

In the town square he found Olaf sitting on the pile of coffins. Nowak was on his knees at the foot of the pile, Lars standing behind him with the muzzle of a handgun pressed to the back of Nowak's neck.

'Cut me some slack, Olaf? For old time's sake? For Grace? All it needed, all it would have taken was some rain. That's all it needed.'

'You wanted it rain, you should've come see me, Nowak.'

As Olaf spoke, a cloud passed over the sun. Nowak raised his face to the sky.

'I said it would rain,' he shouted. 'I told them the rain would come. I knew it would come.'

'You wanted it rain, you should've come see me,' Olaf said again.

Without warning, Monk stepped forward and, in a single movement, raised his revolver to Nowak's temple and blew his brains out. The noise jolted Lars and in the same instant he put another round through the back of Nowak's neck, severing his spinal column so that Nowak's head skewed impossibly as his torso hit the ground. Monk pushed Lars aside and fired five more rounds into Nowak's head, obliterating his face, turning his skull into a pulp of white and grey and red.

SIX

ON THE IMPORTANCE OF SURPRISE WHEN ATTACKING THE ENEMY

1985. Oil on canvas. 125.1 × 108.1 cm. The death of Balder including self-portrait as Hod. Artist's private collection.

NOTES: This stylised interpretation of the death of Balder ('The Glorious', also called the god of tears) at the unwitting hands of his twin the blind god Hod ('War', god of winter) superimposes the face of Lars Janssen on to that of Balder and the artist's own on to that of Hod, reflecting a deeply felt survivor's guilt on the part of the artist after Janssen's death in 1980. The sensual and often overtly sexual imagery in the work is used to reflect the fact that the dart of mistletoe with which Balder was murdered has modern connotations of love and makes an incongruous, yet curiously fitting weapon with which to kill an otherwise invulnerable god. In the myth Hod was subsequently killed by a young giant and son of Odin called Vali, but in Monk's interpretation a barely decipherable inscription appears in the bottom right of the work: 'The giants are gone: there is no angel to avenge and none to mourn the death of the god of tears.'

Claude Tartaro, Page 152.

One Friday afternoon in August the curator of the Republic's art collection and godfather to the wealthiest non-identical twins on the planet sat in the north-west corner of the Exchequer Room of the Republic on Russia Street in west London, a corner coveted for its proximity in summer to a window and in winter to the huge fireplace set in the west wall. The clock on the wall behind the bar of steel and black-stained wood which extended along fully half of the Exchequer Room's south wall had begun to disintegrate harmoniously. It was twenty-three minutes and forty-four seconds to five. Forty-three. Forty-two. Forty-one. Forty.

Charles Monk shifted uncomfortably in his new armchair. He had eaten well in the Republic's restaurant: an English lunch of calf's brains in black butter; a mixed grill of liver and kidneys and steak, skuets; an eel pie, roast potatoes and greens and swede mash and gravy, all washed down with stout ale and champagne; then gooseberry tart and a great deal of cream. And now he had drunk port and coffee and smoked a cigar.

A fresh breeze had begun to billow the drapes. Clouds were gathering. Twenty-five. Twenty-four. Twenty-three.

Miriam had looked at him differently afterwards. He did not know if Lars had ever told her what happened, and she had never asked him, but she saw the difference in him.

The scars on his face, the misshapen nose, the shattered cheekbones and jaw served to hide the changes from most people, but she saw them and they seduced her.

In nineteen-sixty-eight Lars had asked him to paint her.

'She's so beautiful now, Monk. I want her beauty captured while she's still young.'

He wanted a full-length nude. Miriam was reluctant, but Lars insisted. It was not as if Monk had never seen her naked, he said, and besides, no one else would ever see it. It would hang in their stateroom on the *Ringhorn*, where no one else was permitted to go.

She was in Paris studying at the Sorbonne. Monk rented a studio. It was May.

She kissed him on each cheek, took his hand and led him to the sofa by the window, sat beside him. The room at sunset had the sepia half-tones of an old photograph. He fixed it in his mind.

'Good room,' he said.

'Of course. Did you think he would let me live as a student?'

'He's worried about you. The riots.'

'He'd be even more worried if he knew who I stood beside last night on the barricades.'

'I won't tell him.'

'I'll tell him soon enough. But after. Just to shock him.'

'Aha! At last someone who believes there will be an "after". Sartre seems to think this is it. The revolution.'

'Sartre.'

'You don't admire him?'

'No.'

'It was interesting, though. To sketch him. He was fascinated by the mechanics of it. It was like giving an art lesson to someone. It was difficult to make him sit still, he kept wanting to look.'

'It's his vanity. And that's why I don't admire him. But I met de Beauvoir last month. I admire her.'

'And your studies?'

'Yes. Perhaps I will do a doctorate. We'll see.'

'And Lars?'

'You haven't seen him?'

'I was only in Tangiers for a day. He was in New York. I haven't spoken to him properly for months. Since he made me agree to this.'

'I told him he must not visit me here. He was very unhappy about it, but I think it must happen.'

'You don't miss him?'

'Of course. But he is too like a brother to me and he still sees me like his little sister instead of as his wife. I have to become a woman and he has to see the difference, you understand?'

'Yes. Does he?'

'He's very jealous, but I'm a good girl. Anyway, it suits me to be contrary. They're all out there talking about free love and here I am, the celibate academic. They tease me, but they are like sheep.'

'Yes. They are sheep.'

'I like to mystify them.'

Monk reached out and stroked her hair. She took his hand, squeezed gently.

'I have a bottle of red wine from Bordeaux. Would you like to drink some?'

'Or I could take you out somewhere for a meal, perhaps.'

'Everywhere is closed. I have bread and cheese and wine. And do you like to smoke these?'

She offered him a Gauloise.

'No, I have Luckies.'

'You will become an American and we will all hate you.'

She poured a glass of wine for each of them.

'*Et l'Indochine?*'

'Wet. Beautiful. You must go there one day.'

'Was it horrible?'

'I was at Khe Sanh for four weeks. My ears are still ringing. It's strange, to walk on the streets and not hear properly. It's like being in a dream, or a film.'

'And when the picture is done? What will you do then.'

'Go back there. Olaf has given me an aeroplane.'

'He's generous.'

'He has reason to be.'

'*C'est vrai. Et ton père?*'

'He's bought a big house in the country. A manor house with mill ponds. The mill ponds are stocked with carp. He spends a lot of time fishing.'

'I would like to see him again soon. Perhaps I will visit him this summer. We could go together.'

'I must work.'

'Yes, work. There is always work.'

The weeks passed in a blur of politics and wine and the strange torture of spending hour upon hour studying her body, tracing every contour, exploring every shadow. She teased him.

'They all think you are with me. I tell them it isn't so, but they don't believe me. Poor Charlie. You can't have me and they won't have you because they think you can.'

'*Allez, la musique,*' he said.

She laughed.

Her friends disliked him at first. They opposed the war. He did not.

'War promotes honesty,' he said at a dinner party one night. 'Or perhaps war is a form of honesty. If we cannot have honesty, what can we have?'

They took him seriously. They persuaded themselves of his arguments.

'We must wage war in pursuit of the truth!' one of them shouted as they rolled out into the night.

'The only truth is pleasure!' shouted another.

'We must wage war in pursuit of pleasure!' a third.

'They are crazy,' she said when they were gone.

It was her idea to spend the evening naked together. It was to be his last night in Paris. In the morning they would fly to London where Lars was working in the City office of Janssen Shipping. They would unveil the portrait to him.

'How can I explain why? You have made me into an object for this last month. Now I want to be me again. I want to be a person to you. This is my way.'

Still he could barely bring himself to look at her.

He had drunk absinthe, the wormwood jackhammering his brain until the world was magnesium-haloed and crystalline. She drank red wine. Her breath turned to honey, glued itself to whatever it touched, dripped from the walls and coated the floor.

The pieces of the clock on the wall behind the bar were starting to rattle gently. A sure sign of weather on the way, Buck Rogers would say. It was twenty minutes and thirty seconds to five. Twenty-nine. Twenty-eight. Twenty-seven.

There was the rumble of distant thunder.

They all bore scars, nursed wounds. It was Buck Rogers who was most deeply affected by the affair, having seen Nowak's treatment of her at first hand during his weeks of playing El Ojo in Nowak's film.

Janssen Shipping lawyers quickly established that she was an orphan, a ward of the Italian state though she was British born and bred. Childless himself, Rogers became her legal guardian; he installed her in a flat in Paris in the same block as Miriam's own apartment so she could keep an eye on the girl and report back. Rogers visited when he could but she remained remote from him, from everyone. Monk did not see her except once, on the morning that he and Miriam had left Paris for London to unveil Lars's painting to him. She had seen him, locked eyes with him, then gone on her way without a word.

They tried sending her to psychiatrists but she would refuse to speak, except to tell them her name was Galatea, Gala if they preferred. Rogers's visits grew less frequent, though he spoke of her often, spoke to Monk often, demanding details of Nowak's death. Tell it again, Short Order, he would say and Monk would sigh and describe once more how it had been. And how did it feel, Short Order? How did it feel to blow that fucker's brains out?

Monk drew the line at painting the scene from memory.

In nineteen-seventy she disappeared. No one knew exactly when, but it was after her eighteenth birthday in April and before the end of June when Buck Rogers, concerned by the fact that her telephone had been cut off and that he had heard nothing from her in months, travelled to Paris to see her. He found her apartment empty, no furniture, nothing.

'Are you sure you killed that son of a bitch, Short Order?' he asked.

'I'm sure,' Monk had said.

The full resources of Janssen Shipping were thrown into the search. Detective agencies were hired in every country of the world: discreet enquiries, no fuss to be made, but find her, just make sure she's OK.

It was as if she had never existed.

The private detectives watched Kurt Nowak for months: nothing. Rogers visited him and asked him outright.

'Kurt Nowak might be lowlife faggot scum, but he doesn't know where she is now. I'm sure of that,' Rogers said.

Monk was in Cambodia at the time. Keep an eye out for her, Rogers said on the phone one day, the irony lost on him that not a day went past when Monk did not see her face, fleetingly, impossibly, wherever he went, as she was when he had first set eyes on her: no more than eleven, twelve years old, tall for her age but with the body of a child, dirty cheeks streaked with tears, defiance in the set of her mouth but fear tugging at her lower lip.

'Sure, Buck,' he said. 'I'll keep my eyes open.'

She was not to be found. Rogers travelled to Spain, to Fuego-Fire. Nothing. Eventually he gave up the search, but one summer on the *Ringhorn* Monk and Rogers stayed up late in his ready room off the bridge.

'She won't let me go, Short Order,' Rogers said. 'One day she'll turn up like the bad penny she is. I might be long gone, but one day she'll turn up. You promise me you'll take care of her, Short Order? You promise me that?'

'I promise, Buck.'

In nineteen-eighty the *Ringhorn* caught fire. An explosion holed her. She sank within minutes, all hands lost. Monk heard the news on the World Service, was whisked from Pakistan to England in a CIA Lear jet. The children were playing in the grounds of his father's house when he arrived. As he watched them play, he cried: the only time. His father: 'I like having them around. They can stay and I'll see to the business for now.'

When his father died in nineteen-eighty-four the children stayed on at the house, cared for by George Monk's housekeeper and lover Mrs Dee, but she had no head for business. Monk took a cursory look at the books and appointed a caretaker manager whose brief was to do nothing: buy nothing, sell nothing, just keep it ticking over until the twins are old enough to take control.

There was a hole in the accounts. The manager queried it with Monk, millions being taken every year from a numbered Swiss account drawing against the Janssen Shipping ledger. Monk said he would look into it, assumed a throwback to Olaf's time when cash would appear and disappear as if with a life of its own. He decided to wait and see.

In nineteen-eighty-five Janssen Shipping made a loss for the first time in its history. Something had to be done. Monk pulled strings. The account was owned by an offshore trust based in Gibraltar. Monk pulled strings. The Janssen family representative on the board of trustees was Miriam Janssen. No one had told them she was dead. Monk pulled strings.

Then he flew to Spain, to Granada, hired a Land-Rover and a trail bike and borrowed a revolver from a friend of a friend. Then he drove into the mountains.

The road into the mountains began as a sweeping brushstroke across the landscape of the foothills. By the time it reached the mesa it should have been a scrabbling hypoxic track: someone had paved the way. The road was narrow but passable in the Land-Rover. He drove through the night. It was dawn by the time he arrived.

At the top of a low rise a huge, brightly-painted sign spanned the tarmac:

BIENVENIDO EN FUEGO
WELCOME TO FIRE

And from beneath the sign the town was visible. Monk stopped the engine and got out of the Land-Rover.

A wide boulevard was lined with tall wooden buildings; narrow sidestreets made a ragged edge to the east, west and north; and to the south there was a gradual metamorphosis from western frontier style to that of a Mexican pueblo: whitewashed walls, a large church with a bell-tower, goats and chickens roaming the streets. And beyond the town, on a low hill, there was a graveyard surrounded by a white picket fence and, above the graveyard entrance, a flashing neon sign. Through his binoculars Monk could make out the words: *The End of the Road*.

He got back into the Land-Rover, field stripped the

borrowed revolver and loaded it, left it close to hand, lit a cigar. Then he drove to the edge of town, parked the Land-Rover, slipped the revolver into the waistband of his jeans and walked along the main drag towards the town square where, he could see, a scaffold had been built and something corpse-shaped hung from a hangman's noose, swinging gently in the breeze.

The town was deserted, a ghost town, but not quite dead. From a saloon there was the sound of music and laughter and glasses clinking. Monk went in. There was no one there, the sounds piped in through hidden speakers. From the livery stables, the noise of a blacksmith hammering iron. There was no blacksmith, no horses, just hay. A whore's laughter echoed from an empty room in the hotel.

As he neared the town square the object hanging from the gallows became clear. It was a skeleton dressed in a black tailcoat, dress trousers, brogues. Monk climbed the scaffold to take a closer look: plastic: Made in Hong Kong.

Where he had once drunk whisky with Olaf and Lars and Jean-Louis Nowak, she had built a cinema. *KINO* flashed over the entrance in letters four feet high. He went in. Buck Rogers's face leered at him from the screen. Rogers lifted his eyepatch to reveal, in place of an eyeball, a socket filled with polished gold.

'Please don't hurt him,' Gala said to El Ojo's back.

Monk watched the movie. It ended abruptly, no credits, then opened almost immediately: permanent loop. He watched it again, just to be sure. It was only half-an-hour long.

*

He stayed for three days, exploring the town, looking for
signs of life, for her, hoping she would come. He left her a
note on the reception desk of the hotel where he had slept:
Please spend less. – CM.

Monk ordered another schnapps. It was eighteen minutes and thirty-seven seconds to five. Thirty-six. Thirty-five. Thirty-four. Thirty-three.

Monk's schnapps came. He sipped from the glass. There was a flash of lightning and a few moments later a rumble of thunder.

A few splashes of rain hit the windowsill. Henri made as if to close the windows but Monk waved him away.

There was a war on. Monk spent the rest of nineteen-eighty-five in Honduras. She would not let him go. In England for Christmas he painted her from memory. The work was kitsch and shit. He destroyed it. In the spring he travelled again to Spain, spent a week in the town. She was there, he knew, because each morning he would walk to the graveyard and each morning he would find freshly cut flowers on the real graves. On all the real graves but one: where Jean-Louis Nowak lay the earth was bare.

She would not let him go. Every year for the next ten years he travelled to Spain. Sometimes for a day or two, sometimes for a week, once for three months. She never let herself be seen, but she would leave him gifts, always made sure the room he stayed in at the hotel was aired, the bedlinen clean.

It was nineteen-eighty-seven when the first people came.

Monk arrived to find them living in the Mexican district: bohemian types, artists and musicians, a poet or two, ageing Convoy remnants, elastic-faced and mostly not all there. They knew who he was, left him alone.

A year later the hotel had staff. A receptionist banged a bell and a bellhop carried his bags to his room before he could even open his mouth. There was a queue to enter the cinema and tourists were being charged five hundred pesetas to see Jean-Louis Nowak's unfinished masterpiece as often as they liked in one sitting. The girl at the till waved him in for free.

One night he got drunk and picked a fight with a hippie musician from Berlin. He was arrested and spent the night in jail. The sheriff was William Matthews. Monk had met him before and feared the worst. Matthews was a former mob enforcer whose most chilling boast was that he had never killed a man in his life. Monk believed this to be true, though he knew for a fact that half-a-dozen of Matthews's victims had taken their own lives after receiving his attention.

Matthews made the most of his captive audience and talked at Monk until late into the night.

'You know, Charles, Fuego was never a lawless town any more than it was ever simply a film set or a theme park. Of course, it was a film set and there's something of a theme park feel to it now, but lawless? Never. And certainly not while William Matthews is the sheriff around here. It's not a bad job to have, Charles, and I've got a gift for it, for keeping order in places where, shall we say, the reach of government doesn't quite extend. I have the full confidence of my beautiful wife. She doesn't want to see you hurt, Charles, but she allows me a certain licence. So I would ask you to conduct yourself with the dignity befitting your station in life, you understand me now?'

He banged the bars of the cell with his night stick. His voice rose to a sudden shout.

'I will not tolerate assaults on anyone here. Do you understand me, Charles?'

Monk had nodded. He understood. He moved to the bars and gripped them. The door to the cell swung slightly open.

'Are there no locks in this town?' he asked.

Matthews simply fixed him with a cold, unsmiling stare. Monk understood, remembered. Even in Fuego's jail, locks were not needed.

His dreams that night were of steel slicing through skin, of the long moments before blood begins to well.

In the morning the sheriff charged tourists for entry: a real live jailbird for all to see. She came, her head wrapped in a shawl, a scarf over her nose and mouth, dark glasses hiding her eyes.

'Well well well,' she said. 'If it isn't Charlie Monk.'

Then she laughed that extraordinary, throaty, abandoned laugh and Monk could do nothing but smile and shake his head.

Janssen Shipping's business manager complimented Monk on his financial nous. The investment, whatever it was, was showing good returns. She sent Monk a note. I pay my debts. – G.

In nineteen-eighty-nine when Xavier and Francine were sixteen Monk took them there.

'We own this?' Francine asked.

'It's a long story,' Monk said. 'I'll tell you it one day.'

The sheriff asked Francine if she would open the new hospital.

'My wife insists,' he said.

The hospital was named for Miriam. The opening was unconventional: a magnum of champagne smashed against a whitewashed wall.

'What was that about?' Xavier asked.

'Later,' said Monk. 'I'll explain later.'

'And who's his wife?' Francine asked.

'Later,' said Monk. 'I'll explain later.'

They stayed for the summer. It was the longest Monk had ever spent with his godchildren. He taught them to ride and to shoot. Xavier wanted to learn how to make bombs. Monk refused. Francine wanted to learn how to hot-wire a car. Monk taught her. She spent a week joyriding in the desert until the sheriff arrested her and put her in jail. She sulked for three days until she discovered that she enjoyed being watched. She performed tricks and dances and songs for the tourists. One of them was a photographer. He said she could be a model and she agreed to do a photoshoot in the desert when she was free. The sheriff released her early on grounds of good behaviour. The shoot was a success. She made the cover of *marie claire*.

Xavier taught himself to make bombs. He spent his days blowing up rocks. Monk decided to teach him to make them properly before he blew himself up. They spent their days blowing up larger rocks with sticks of homemade dynamite. The sheriff threatened to arrest them both unless they stopped. They stopped. The sheriff taught them how to break locks and crack safes and gave Xavier anatomy lessons. They agreed that it was more fun than blowing up rocks.

When it was time to leave, Xavier and Francine wanted to stay. Monk told them why Fuego had been built and rebuilt. They changed their minds.

'Your grandfather was a bad man. You just have to learn to live with that,' Monk said.

'We should give it away,' said Francine. 'All of it.'

'That's up to you, but until you're eighteen it's yours. You have no choice.'

'You can give your half away,' Xavier said. 'But I'm keeping mine.'

The storm was all around them now. Lightning forked and seared into the earth, near-instantaneous cracks of thunder rattled the windowframes. The rain was mixed with hail which was being driven by the wind through the open windows of the Exchequer Room to skitter across the wooden floor, a thousand random drum rolls to serenade the day.

Still Monk would not allow Henri to close the windows.

In nineteen-ninety-one Xavier and Francine came of age. Francine's catwalk name was Franny: Salinger fan extraordinaire, geek heroine, heroin-chic chick with a habit to match, loft in New York, gracing the arms of a string of pop stars, actors and tennis players. The tennis players were the worst. Monk picked fights with them, argued with her. Reconciliation would be a long time in coming.

Xavier wanted to run the business. He pumped Monk for history. Monk gave him Olaf's old address book, kept safe at George Monk's manor house for all these years. He never dreamt that Xavier would use it.

'I want to reopen the club,' Xavier said. 'I don't know why you closed it.'

'I'm an artist, not a businessman. Think yourself lucky there's anything left at all.'

'There might as well not be for all there is.'

A cheap shot and not quite true, but Monk had let things slide and the Janssen family billions were millions now, Janssen Shipping no longer a player. Xavier saw it as a challenge.

They went to the Republic together. Beetle larvae had attacked the wooden floors and furniture, cobwebs hung thick from the ceiling and over the windows, damp had set in where guttering had fallen into disrepair, a fine layer of dust covered every surface. Half-full ashtrays and empty glasses, even plates of food were still on tables, left as they were on the day the place closed down. Monk picked up a menu, handed it to Xavier.

'What?'

'Souvenir,' Monk said.

The ruin was not terminal. It would be Xavier's first venture before taking control of Janssen Shipping and turning the company around.

'I kind of like it as it is,' he said.

'So keep it as it is,' Monk said. 'Just fix the damp.'

'And a new bar. It needs a new bar.'

Monk agreed to furnish works of art and oversee the design. Francine signed up celebrity members in their droves. The club was a success.

Xavier moved on to bigger things: a five-year orgy of Swedish can-do and business globetrot took Janssen Shipping temporarily back to its roots: Rangoon, Cali, Miami, Palermo, Hong Kong: sons and grandsons of friends of Olaf Janssen happy to do business even with an eighteen-year-old punk with water behind his ears, the word on the street that Sweet William was back on the Janssen-family payroll: not something to be taken lightly.

And now Janssen Shipping was no more and Janssen Mercantile (Fund Management) PLC was the new kid on the City block, but so big, so respected, that already it might have been there for a hundred years. Shipping and finance: the perfect synergy, Xavier liked to say. And he and Francine ruling as Isis and Osiris, golden children, orphan king and queen with the world at their feet.

In nineteen-ninety-four Xavier had commissioned a new *Ringhorn*. It would be launched in the autumn, a hundred-metre blue-water superyacht – floating office, castle, temple to ill-gotten wealth. The thought of it made Monk smile even as it weighed on him, the tempting of Providence, the stoking of history's most consuming addiction, its craving for repetition-as-nemesis, the endless reification of age-old myth as the golden son burns again on the pyre of his longship, the blind god's aim ever true.

A few months earlier Xavier had come to him.

'The Fuego gig turns a nice profit, but it's not core business. I want to sell it.'

Monk asked him how much, haggled him down, paid him the sum of one Maria Theresa thaler.

'Out of respect for your mother,' Monk said to him. 'She'd have wanted it to stay in the family.'

'Don't pull that family shit on me, Monk,' Xavier said. 'You just want to keep an eye on the Surgeon, make sure she doesn't send him after you one day.'

He stormed off, irritated by the impunity with which *consigliere* could pull rank on *capo*. The contract arrived in the post the following day. Monk took Xavier out the same night, got him drunk, gave him the coin, given to him in nineteen-sixty-eight as commission for painting Miriam's portrait for Lars: blood money.

Xavier was no better at holding his drink than his father had been. Monk, in no mood to indulge the frailties of the Janssen line, carried him over his shoulder from bar to bar for the rest of the night. Xavier had barely talked to him since. The *paparazzi* shots made the front page of the *Sun*.

SEVEN

The Pain We Cause Others (and the Reasons Why)

1968. Oil on canvas. 122.5 × 93 cm. Buddhist monk in lotus position and on fire. Republic, London.

NOTES: The flames enveloping the burning monk form a cone (koan), drawing our attention to the deeper symbolism of the several acts of self-immolation undertaken by Buddhist monks during this period. Monk frequently declared himself fascinated by the spectacle of these burning monks and cultivated contacts in the monasteries, with the result that he was often informed of self-immolations in advance so he could observe them from beginning to end. He described his own reaction to the burnings as 'a feeling of profound serenity as I watch', but acknowledged that as a form of protest against the war they were probably too subtle for the Western mind to comprehend in any meaningful way.

Claude Tartaro, Page 29.

They had collected him from his room and now they were parked on a street somewhere, they would not tell him where or what time it was. It was raining heavily. Occasionally Grace Matthews would complain about the weather.

'The sooner we get back the better.'

William Matthews just grunted. Tartaro sat in silence.

His biography of Charles Monk had remained untouched as he pursued his modest literary career, but in nineteen-ninety-four he first heard rumours of a bizarre community of bohemians living in a small town high in the Sierra Nevada in southern Spain. He knew instantly that, as speculative as it was, he had to go there. Still cautious about crossing Charles Monk again, he put his affairs in order before leaving Paris by train and travelling, with overnight stops in Barcelona and Madrid, to Granada. There he hired a car and bought a map and obtained vague directions from an American hippie he met in a bar.

The drive into the mountains took the best part of the day and repeatedly Tartaro missed the ever-narrower turn-offs the map showed. As dusk approached he was faced with the choice of sleeping in the car or returning to one of the guest-houses he had passed on his way up. He parked and tested the air temperature. It was cold, colder than he had imagined Spain could be. According to the directions the hippie had given him, the town should be within a couple of miles of this spot, but there was no sign of the road the man had described, or of any habitation at all. Then he saw it, a silvery band of tarmac winding its way through a narrow ravine. The road is on no map, the hippie had said; this road was not marked.

When he arrived in Fuego the town was bathed in light. There were fires burning in the streets and hundreds of people milled around drunkenly, sharing bottles of wine and eating meat from paper plates. He had arrived during their fiesta. He found the hotel and finally got the attention of a receptionist who showed him to a room.

'You're lucky, Señor Tartaro. This is the last free room in the whole town. We saved it for you, and it's one of our best rooms as well. If things keep going like this, La Señora will have to build another hotel.'

'La Señora?'

'All in good time, Señor Tartaro, all in good time.'

He spent the evening on the balcony of his room looking down on the fiesta and resisting invitations to join the crowds on the streets. In the morning he went for a walk, watched Jean-Louis Nowak's unfinished film. It was exactly as he had imagined it would be.

He visited the Jean-Louis Nowak Museum: an empty, whitewashed room which cost two thousand pesetas to enter.

He was eating lunch – freshly slaughtered beef – when the summons came. The town's sheriff, William Matthews, sat down at his table.

'My wife is eager to meet you. You'll join her for dessert and coffee.'

When he was shown into Grace Matthews's private apartment on the top floor of the hotel, his breath was taken away. On the walls there were six of Charles Monk's greatest works.

'They're yours?'

'After a fashion, Mr Tartaro. I'm an admirer of his art, certainly. Why have you come? You have been advised, I believe, of the dangers of pursuing your investigation.'

'He killed Jean-Louis Nowak, didn't he?'

'I wouldn't know. I was locked in a storehouse when it happened. I never even saw his corpse. He'd already dug his own grave and made his own coffin. By the time Kurt let me out, whoever had killed him was gone, and all that was left to do was to fill in the hole.'

'So we'll never know.'

'You will never know and it means nothing to me. He was a rapist of children, Mr Tartaro. Not someone to mourn.'

'Some say you were killed when the Janssens' boat sank.'

'But I was not.'

'Were you on board the boat?'

'When it sank? Of course not. A little before, though. The same day.'

'Tell me, did you ever see Monk's portrait of Miriam Janssen?'

She shook her head.

'It drove Lars quite mad, of course,' she said. 'Miriam told me that he could hardly bear to look at it but could not take his eyes from it half the time. And Miriam believed that it was cursed.'

'Why?'

'I've never seen it. No one is permitted to see it. Only one living person has ever seen it and that is Charles Monk – and even he is not permitted to see it again.'

'You speak of it as if it still exists.'

She said nothing, glanced momentarily at one of the paintings on the wall. Tartaro felt a sudden, breathtaking exhilaration.

'It does still exist. It's here, isn't it?'

She said nothing.

'It's here. You must let me see it.'

'Mr Tartaro, I won't say whether it exists or not. It is none of your concern. I will say that even if it did exist, you would not be permitted to see it. If in any unfortunate event you did see it, I would have William pluck out your eyes. It's quite as simple as that. Do you understand? You have already seen at first hand what William can do with a scalpel. He is an artist with the knife, whatever the species of his subject.'

With that Tartaro was escorted to the door by William Matthews.

That night it was as if the years had been peeled away and he was once more a twenty-year-old student in Paris, his fevered dreams haunted by the face of Miriam Janssen as he tossed and turned in his bed. He awoke in a cold sweat, the sheets drenched. It was growing light. He called room service and ordered coffee which he took on to the balcony to drink. No sooner had he sat down than he saw Grace

Matthews and her husband, both dressed in funereal black and laden with flowers. They were leaving the hotel and walking up the main drag in the direction of the white-fenced cemetery on the low hill overlooking the town.

This was his chance.

He dressed hurriedly and made his way stealthily to the top floor. There had been no locks on the door to Grace Matthews's apartment, just as it seemed there were no locks anywhere in Fuego.

The door opened soundlessly. The lights inside were on. Tartaro moved directly to the painting Grace Matthews had involuntarily glanced at on the previous day. It was the largest of the Monks on the walls and its thick gilded frame would easily conceal another picture hanging behind it.

He lifted the painting away from the wall. Nothing. He picked it off the wall and laid it face down on the floor before him. Taped to the back there was something covered with plain brown wrapping paper. He tore the paper away. His breath caught in his throat. It was as if he had been plunged into an icy sea.

For long minutes he drank in The Image, his gaze repeatedly drawn to Miriam Janssen's accusatory stare.

Then there was the click-clunk of an automatic being cocked. William Matthews spoke from some distance behind him.

'Remain where you are, Mr Tartaro. Now, very carefully, replace the wrapping as best you can.'

Shaking, Tartaro did as he was told.

'Here, cover it with this.'

Matthews slid a newspaper across the floor to him. Tartaro unfolded some sheets and spread them over the painting, obscuring it completely. Then there was a sudden pain and a blinding flash as Matthews struck him on the side of the head, then nothing.

EIGHT

4.669

1989. Oil on wood. 85.6 × 69.1 cm. Portrait of Chinese student with butterfly painted or tattooed on face. Private collection.

NOTES: A lifelong opponent of communism, Monk was twice deported from China during the Tiananmen Square demonstrations of 1989, and twice returned. The student model for *4.669* was subsequently tried and executed. Title, which refers to a numerical constant discovered by American mathematician Mitchell Feigenbaum and relating to the then popular field of Chaos Theory, is reflected in the image of the butterfly which in turn represents the oft-quoted Chaos Theory maxim that 'a butterfly stirring the air today in Peking can transform the storm systems next month in New York' (James Gleick). After the fall of the Berlin Wall and the dismantling of communism in the former Soviet Union, Monk frequently referred to *4.669* and the events in Tiananmen Square, suggesting that the students had done more to destroy communism in the Soviet Union than all the political leaders of the West put together.

Claude Tartaro, Page 164.

The clock had finally stopped: quarter-to-five on the dot. The storm was over, the air was fresh. Monk stood and crossed to the painting of Lars, *Maestro*, examined it closely for signs of decay and wear. The colours of the suit of lights were beginning to fade but they would restore well enough.

'I was there, you know.'

Monk turned to face her. She was in the doorway, dressed as a Southern belle. She walked across the room in that same mannered style and sat down. She looked for all the world like a Dix portrait of some society lady come to life.

'It was some party, wasn't it? I spent half the evening talking to Clint Eastwood and the other half making out with William. It was where we first met, you know.'

'Buck looked for you.'

'He looked in the wrong places.'

'What is it you want from me?'

'From you? The courtesy of a drink would be nice but I don't mind buying my own. Champagne, please.'

Monk told Henri to bring a bottle.

'I hear you're my new landlord. Here's to you,' she said, raising her glass, smudging its rim a Revlon-red.

'You keep yourself informed.'

'It was my idea. Don't worry about me, Charlie Monk. I'm rehabilitated. I pissed on that shitheel's grave three times a day every day for the last twenty years. That should do it, don't you think?'

'I can't answer that.'

'It was a rhetorical question. It did it. And you know something? In twenty years up there it never has rained. Some snow, most years, but I never saw a drop of rain fall there. That shitheel had lost it, and he knew it. He wanted Olaf to send someone up to wax him, simple as that. Make him look good. I don't know if it was you or Lars or Olaf himself who pulled the trigger. And frankly I don't give a damn.'

There was a banging sound from the foyer. Gala leapt from her seat and shouted.

'Goddamnit, Bill, be careful with that.'

She sat down again.

'English weather. We've been waiting out in the van for a half-hour just for the rain to stop. You remember Bill, though, don't you?'

'Charles.'

Monk nodded to Matthews. He was holding a wrapped object, the size and shape of a large painting. He propped it against the bar.

'Not over there, Bill, bring it here, prop it up there. Now go get our friend.'

Matthews left the room again.

Monk stood and made as if to cross to the painting.

'Wait up, Charlie Monk. All in good time. First things first – I have a letter for you. I'm sorry it took so long to deliver, but if it helps it wouldn't have helped if you'd got it when you should have. Here.'

He recognised the envelope, the handwriting, the seal. It was from Miriam.

Dear Charlie,

I'm scared. Lars has not been himself since our visit to London. He can't explain it. We had such a wonderful day with you at the club – even he says so – but something must have affected him. For weeks now he keeps asking me about you, about if anything happened with us, about that month in Paris all those years ago. Of course I tell him he is crazy, and it was his idea in the first place, but he is obsessed. He spends many hours each day with the painting, just staring at it, his nose against it at times. I'm worried for him, I'm at a loss. If this reaches you, won't you come and talk to him? I'm sure he would listen to you. I've tried to reach you for a week now, but even your father can't find out where you are. I can't leave Lars for a minute, but I'm giving this to a friend and she'll get it to your father so I hope it reaches you. We changed our minds about touring Amnesia. We're anchored off Gibraltar right now and we'll spend the summer in the Med. You know how to find us.

Lars is calling me, I have to go. Be careful, Charlie. And come soon.
My love,
Miriam.

Monk folded the letter and glanced at Gala.

'I was supposed to get off at Gibraltar,' she told him, 'but Lars wouldn't let us berth. Here's the second one.'

It was on different paper, no envelope. The writing was

scrawled and the ink had run where tears had fallen. It was dated on the day they died.

Dear Charlie,

Lars is much worse. Juliette has locked him in the brig after he took a shotgun from the armoury and shot up the conservatory bar on the sun deck. He's hammering on the door of the brig right now. I'm so scared. Last night he threatened to destroy the painting. I told him to go ahead if it would make him better, but he couldn't do it, held a knife to it but couldn't make himself cut it.

Charlie, I need to explain something. Do you remember Grace – the child actress from Olaf's film?

She's here with me now. I've known all along where she was and what she was doing. She made me promise not to tell Buck; it was difficult but I understand why. His was a fatherly love for her, but there was too much pity in it and I think you will understand that this is insufferable love for someone who has been through what she has. Now that Buck has gone she'll stay on the *Ringhorn* with us for as long as she likes, and I've already set up a bank account for her to use.

Juliette has called a helicopter to come and take Grace off the boat for a few days, just until Lars has calmed down. I'm giving her this letter and the one I wrote yesterday to take to your father. And the painting. Perhaps if it isn't here for a while it will help Lars to get better. Grace has promised she

won't look at it and the wrap is sealed by me. If
Lars thinks others are seeing it he'll only get worse,
but I can't think what else to do.

The helicopter is landing. Please come, Charlie.
Please come soon. We need you here.
My love,
Miriam.

'She should never have got me to take it off the boat,' Gala
said. 'It would have been what tipped him over the edge.'

Monk shook his head, unable to speak as he fingered
the notepaper. He glanced up at the painting.

'Yes,' she said. 'That's it. I suppose I should have
delivered it to your father, but one way or another I got
sidetracked. I promised her I wouldn't look at it, and I
never did.'

'Not once?'

'And I promised her that no one else would look at it,
not even you. That's what they wanted, isn't it?'

Monk nodded.

'It's been back in Fuego all this time. We had a little
accident, though.'

'Tartaro.'

'I blame myself – I must have let something slip. He just
couldn't stop himself. William thought I might want to kill
him there and then, but I still think an eye for an eye was
the right way to go. The question now is what do we do
with him, and what do we do with it?'

NINE

AND ON THE EARTH THERE FELL A CRUEL RAIN

1968. Oil on canvas. 338.4 × 258.1 cm. Nude study of Miriam Janssen. Destroyed.

NOTES: Unseen by anyone except this author, the artist, the subject, and Lars Janssen who commissioned it, work is a full-length nude of Miriam Janssen for which Lars Janssen paid Monk the fee of one Maria Theresa thaler (an Austrian currency unit in common use in parts of North Africa) to complete the painting during a one-month period of intensive sittings in Paris. Subject is portrayed knee deep in a pool, splashing water in the direction of the artist/viewer in an evocation of the myth of Tiresias and Athene. Title is from Camus.

Claude Tartaro, Page 117.

William Matthews led Tartaro across a large wooden floor and sat him down in a deep, comfortable armchair.

Charles Monk was angry and shouting.

'She's dead and gone, for fuck's sake. What does it matter if people see it?'

'I made her a promise, that's what it matters. Listen to me, Charlie Monk. I'll tell you what I told Claude here a couple of years back. If you look at it, I will have William pluck out your eyes. It is as simple as that.'

'Henri!' Monk shouted. 'Build a fire.'

'It's the middle of summer, *chef*.'

There was the slap of a hand against bare flesh and a few moments later Tartaro could hear logs being thrown into a grate.

'I knew you'd see sense, Charlie Monk. And him?'

'Him nothing. You'll leave him here.'

Tartaro felt the heavy, comforting weight of Monk's hand on his shoulder.

'You have nothing to fear from me,' Monk said gently.

Then footsteps receding.

'Put more firelighters in there. I need it hot.'

'Yes, *chef*.'

There was a rustling of paper, then the sound of wrapping being torn.

'Don't do it, Charlie. It's not worth it.'

'Fuck you.'

There was the sound of Matthews cocking his automatic.

'Henri, clear the room. You leave too. No one comes in here until I give the word.'

The sound of people being ushered from their seats, more tearing of paper.

Tartaro felt a sudden jolt, as if an electric charge had been applied directly to his brain. The Image wavered and danced in front of him. Miriam Janssen's features faded in and out of focus. He felt a sudden panic, wanted to shout, could not speak.

Then abruptly The Image was clear again, her eyes as accusatory and pitying and guilty as ever, the eyes of an instantly remorseful Athene, wise beyond the understanding of man and as flawed in her wisdom as only the gods can be.

Grace Matthews sighed, defeated.

'So be it,' she said after a few moments. 'Now place it on the fire. Face down, please.'

'In a minute,' Monk said. 'Just give me one minute.'

Then the acrid smell of oil paint smoking, a sizzling and crackling. The Image seemed to flare with an inner light. Tartaro heard Miriam Janssen's sudden intake of breath, heard the splash of her hand as it struck the water, felt the hot drops of liquid spatter his skin, burn his eyes. He blinked furiously, shaking away the tears. Then slowly The Image returned, its clarity yet greater, its luminosity yet stronger.

Her expression had changed. There was no longer accusation, pity, guilt in her eyes. She was standing upright, proud and yet humble, a smile playing on her lips, the ironic smile of a woman at one with the ephemerality of her physical beauty, but the knowing smile of a woman whose inner beauty was understood as universal, imperishable, a thing beyond the indignities of death and art and right or wrong.

It seemed to Tartaro that she beckoned to him, that when he did not, could not move, she waded towards him, reached out to him. He shook his head. No, he wanted to say. It's not me you want. Her strength was like nothing he had ever known. Effortlessly she pulled him from his seat, drew him into the water. It lapped at his ankles, his shins, his knees, his thighs. Suddenly she laughed.

'Charlie,' she said. 'I knew you'd come. Come on,' she said. 'Come on in.'

Tartaro felt the heavy, comforting weight of Monk's hand on his shoulder, and on his other shoulder the touch of Lars Janssen's fingertips – a light, reassuring grip.

He turned and gazed back at the water's edge, watched the Exchequer Room begin to petrify: the armchair he had sat in, the gun in William Matthews' hand, the bar, the floor, the walls and the paintings hanging on them, all turning to stone under Medusa's baleful glare. And then a sudden crack as the world itself shuddered and crumbled to dust and the four of them were left to bathe and laugh and dance.